A Voice in the Distance

tabitha suzuma

DEFINITIONS

A VOICE IN THE DISTANCE
A DEFINITIONS BOOK 978 1 862 30355 3

First published in Great Britain by Definitions,
an imprint of Random House Children's Books
A Random House Group Company

This edition published 2008

3 5 7 9 10 8 6 4 2

Set in New Baskerville

Definitions are published by Random House Children's Books,
61–63 Uxbridge Road, London W5 5SA

www.**kidsatrandomhouse**.co.uk
www.randomhouse.co.uk

Addresses for companies within The Random House Group Limited
can be found at: www.randomhouse.co.uk/offices.htm

THE RANDOM HOUSE GROUP Limited Reg. No. 954009

A CIP catalogue record for this book is available from the British Library.

Printed and bound by CPI Group (UK) Ltd, Croydon, CR0 4YY

Also by Tabitha Suzuma:

A Note of Madness

From Where I Stand

A Voice in the Distance

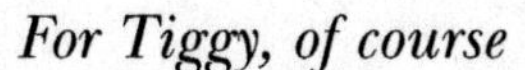

For Tiggy, of course

Acknowledgements

I would like to express my deepest thanks to: Tansy Suzuma for her help and encouragement, Thalia Suzuma for never mincing her words, my mother for her time and effort, Akiko Hart for her support and friendship, Jonathan Middleton for his musical expertise, Adrian Vos for his medical expertise, Linda Davis for her patience, Tracey Paris for another superb cover, Sophie Nelson for her eye for detail, Clare Argar for her hard work, Charlie Sheppard for her edits and her friendship, and of course Tiggy Suzuma for the music.

Chapter One

JENNAH

'Chuck me the tea towel, would you? Not that one, it's wet. The one by the kettle. Thanks. Are you sure we've got enough glasses?'

Harry shoots me an exasperated look as he grapples with the bottle opener. 'D'you want me to count them again?'

'No. I'll just put these ones out too. Oh God, they're filthy.'

'Here, give them to me,' Harry says firmly. 'Now will you just sit down and have a drink?'

'I can't get drunk till everything's sorted,' I protest. 'Otherwise dinner won't even happen. Where have you put the cake?'

'On the table. We're short of three candles but I'm sure Flynn won't be counting.'

I move across to the adjoining living room to examine the table for the umpteenth time. Some of the wineglasses look decidedly streaky and the tablecloth badly needs ironing. The sideboard and a small table have been pushed together to create one long table.

My mother would remark that the cutlery is in need of a good polish. We had to borrow some extra plates from the downstairs neighbour and two of them are decorated with Beatrix Potter characters. The cake looks positively lopsided and the icing seems to be turning orange. I suddenly feel exhausted.

'Here.' Harry hands me a glass of red wine as I sink down onto the sofa. 'It's going to be fine, Jen.'

I fiddle anxiously with the stem of my glass. 'What if everyone's late? What if Flynn gets here first?'

'No one's going to be late,' Harry tries to reassure me. 'Everyone knows it's a surprise party.'

I leave Harry to tend to the goulash and go into the bedroom to get changed. As usual, the mess is not mine: Flynn's jeans, T-shirts and hoodies are strewn over the carpet, musical scores spilling off our shared desk. My clothes land on top of the overflowing laundry basket and I wriggle into a black dress I bought during the summer holidays but never got round to wearing. Too tight – oh, no. The blue dress instead? No time. Stockings to hide pasty legs; high heels have disappeared, only Flynn's trainers are under the bed. OK, shoes last, move on to the bathroom. Soap in eyes, ouch. Front of dress, soaked. Flyaway hair – up or down? Up. Hairgrip won't grip. Now I look like I've been dragged backwards through a bush. Hairgrip back out, start again—

'Jennah, we're short of two chairs!' Harry calls from the kitchen.

Can't talk, hairgrip in mouth. Grunt instead.

'Jennah!'

Spit out hairgrip. 'The swivel chair in the bedroom!'

Hair finally done, still too wispy – it'll have to do. Make-up. Face not dry, mascara blots. The sound of Harry dragging the chair down the corridor. 'We're still one short.'

'Piano stool,' I call back. Blusher or no blusher? No need, already look like a stressed-out tomato. The buzzer goes. Already? I find my shoes underneath Flynn's music bag and shove them on, turning my ankle as I attempt to run for the door.

When I finally limp back to the living room, Kate is there, throwing streamers across the tablecloth. 'I brought decorations,' she says. 'Oh wow, you look stunning, Jen. Is that a new dress?'

'Newish.' I give Kate a quick kiss on the cheek. 'How are you? I'm stressed.'

'Don't be stressed. The table looks beautiful and the food smells great. Breathe!' Kate commands.

'Why are you hobbling?' Harry asks as I go over to the stove to check on the goulash.

'I think I sprained my ankle.'

'Doing what?'

'Putting on my shoes.'

Harry and Kate start to laugh.

'Do you want me to cut up the bread?' Kate asks.

'Yes please. Thank you. God, the table looks like a bar.'

'I told you we didn't need all these glasses,' Harry says.

'But some of them are bound to get broken,' I point out.

'Jennah the eternal optimist!' Harry teases.

The buzzer goes again and the small flat begins to fill. Harry and Kate are doing the drinks. I return to the relative calm of the kitchen to taste my goulash, burning my mouth. I wonder, not for the first time today, what will happen if all the food turns out to be inedible. I suppose, as Harry kindly pointed out earlier, that there is always bread and cheese. In the room next door, the stereo bursts into life and it sounds as if the evening is underway. I check my watch. All we need now is the birthday boy. And if he has any inkling of what is in store for him, he is likely to do a no-show.

I think I have done a pretty good job of keeping things under wraps. I did the shopping in the morning and then dropped it off at Harry's so as not to give the game away with a fully-stocked fridge. As arranged, a mate from uni, André, swung by in the early evening to take Flynn out for a birthday drink. As soon as the coast was clear I called Harry, who drove round with a car-load of extra stools and chairs, some tablecloths from his mum's linen closet and five bulging supermarket bags. The last two hours have been a cooking frenzy and now I feel wiped out and the party hasn't even begun.

Harry comes in backwards through the swing doors

that separate the kitchen from the living room carrying three bottles of wine. 'More booze,' he says. 'I'll put these ones in the fridge.'

'Are there enough thingies out there?' I ask him, rapidly peeling some potatoes.

'You need to be more specific, Jen.'

'Snacks.'

'Masses.'

'Is everyone here?'

'Yes. And André's just texted to say they're on their way. You couldn't have timed it better. People are here, food is ready' – he stirs the goulash, prods the meat and turns down the heat – 'now all we need is the hostess.' He grabs me round the waist and pulls me firmly away from the stove. Before we reach the swing doors, I stop him, laughing suddenly. 'Are we crazy or what?'

'Flynn's never going to forgive us,' Harry agrees with a grin.

As we go out into the living room, the buzzer goes. Kate answers. She gestures frantically at everyone to hush. Someone turns off the music and everyone stops talking. The overheated room vibrates with silent, repressed energy. Kate leaves the front door ajar and retreats quickly to the back of the room, out of the line of fire. There are voices from the stairwell outside. The room collectively holds its breath . . .

'SURPRISE!'

Flynn looks as if he has been punched in the stomach. Hard. Oh God, please smile. There is a deafening silence as we all wait for his look of shock to turn to one of joy. It doesn't happen. Harry bounds to the rescue. 'Happy birthday, old man!' He gives Flynn a hearty slap on the back and hands him a drink.

'Jesus,' Flynn says softly, accepting his drink, and manages something that could pass for a smile. The tension breaks as people come forward to greet him: André is talking about how he nearly gave the game away and everyone starts chatting again and the music is switched back on. I allow myself to breathe. Caught in a group with André and Harry and a couple of uni people, Flynn begins to look a fraction less horrified and my heart rate starts to drop. Relieved, I gulp at my drink and am able to laugh with Kate.

'I wasn't sure who he looked ready to kill first, you or Harry!' she is saying.

'I'm going to say it was all Harry's idea!'

'Watch out,' Kate warns. 'Harry will be blaming it all on you.'

I laugh and serve up the goulash, and top up people's drinks and take the second batch of sausage rolls out of the oven and mop up the contents of an overturned wineglass. I am introduced to somebody's girlfriend and to somebody's brother, then an annoying trombonist called Andy starts talking to me about perfect syncopations. I watch Flynn covertly from across the room. He looks as if he is smiling through gritted teeth. He is talking to an organist – Holly something – who keeps flicking her long plume of hair into his face, causing him to nervously jerk his head back each time. I am amused because rumour has it that Holly fancies Flynn, even though he is blissfully unaware. A lot of girls at the Royal College fancy Flynn, especially now that he has begun to make a name for himself on the competition circuit. He was known as 'that crazy Finnish pianist' for a while after news got round about his bipolar disorder, but that has faded from most people's minds now.

When I eventually manage to extract myself from Andy, I dive back into the kitchen to open some more bottles of wine and meet Harry over the kitchen table.

'All right? Less stressed now? The food's going down well,' he says.

I manage a smile. 'Yeah, it's going OK, isn't it? Has Flynn got over the shock?'

'A few more drinks and he'll be fine.' Harry grins.

We return to the other room and somebody cranks up the music and a few people start to dance and I sink onto the arm of the sofa, utterly spent. Someone trips over my foot and someone else half falls into my lap and the smell of hash mingles with the smell of cigarette smoke and I try to have a conversation with Kate by yelling in her ear. I am just relieved we had the foresight to invite all the people in the building. Harry comes over and squeezes onto the sofa. Kate snuggles up against him and closes her eyes.

'Where's the birthday boy snuck off to then?' Nadim, a percussionist, shouts to me over Harry's head.

I shrug and perform a quick scan of the room, realizing I haven't seen Flynn for a while.

'Are you planning on getting up for orchestra rehearsal tomorrow morning?' Harry yells in my ear.

'Hardly!' I yell back.

'Old Riley's going to have a fit when half the members of the orchestra pull a sickie!' Harry laughs.

'Don't care, I've got my excuse!' I shout.

'What's that then?'

'Sore thumb.' I waggle it. My flute has been gathering dust on the shelf for nearly a week now.

'Due to . . . ?'

'RSI – repetitive strain injury,' I reply. 'Otherwise known as overwork. Not something you would know much about, Harry,' I tease. Harry is known to practise the cello for as little as two hours a day.

'Laugh as much as you want, but next year I'll be making millions writing the score for the next James Bond film, while you and Flynn tour the country as struggling musicians!'

I thump him, narrowly missing Kate. 'No way! You got the place on the Music Tech MA?'

Harry grins. 'Yeah. The letter arrived this morning.'

'Harry, that's fantastic!'

Harry nods. 'Must admit it's a relief to know what I'll be doing after finals.'

'Tell me about it. My mum's been going on at me all year about applying for jobs.'

'Flynn hasn't managed to persuade you to

accompany him on his little jaunt round Europe then?' Harry asks, referring to the concert bookings Flynn has lined up for after we graduate.

I give a rueful smile. 'I have my life too, Harry.'

'Of course, of course. I just meant . . . he'll be lost without you, Jen.' Harry gives me a wink.

'There are the holidays,' I point out. 'And if I manage to save some money over the summer, I should be able to fly out to a couple of his concerts.'

'Yeah, I'm definitely going to try and make the Berlin one,' Harry said. 'Thank God for EasyJet.' He holds Kate's head against his chest as he leans forwards to grab a bottle of red from the coffee table. 'More wine, Jen? Kate's out for the count. Maybe I should take her home.'

'You can't go yet – we haven't even had the birthday cake,' I protest, peeling myself off the sofa. 'I'll go and light the candles.'

I borrow someone's lighter and steady myself against the side of the table as I begin lighting the candles. There seem to be hundreds of them all of a sudden. I realize I'm drunk – thanks to Harry's top-ups and the fact that I haven't got round to eating much today. I drop the lighter onto the cake, then burn my little finger trying to retrieve it. Ellen, a fellow flautist, kindly offers to help. I hand her the lighter. 'Where the hell's Flynn?'

'He went off ages ago,' Ellen replies. 'We thought the two of you had gone out somewhere.'

'No, I've been sitting here the whole time,' I protest,

suddenly annoyed. 'Oh, this is great! So now I'm supposed to blow out the candles for him?' I move away from Ellen, taking a bite of French bread to try and soak up some of the alcohol, and hurry out into the corridor, kicking off my tottery shoes as I go.

Somebody is throwing up in the bathroom. I leave them to it and continue on down towards the bedroom. I open the door and fumble for the light switch but can't find it. I trip over a large pile of coats and bags spilling off the end of the bed. Cursing, I pick myself up off the floor. The curtains are open, revealing a tall pane of black night. From the light coming in off the street, I can make out a figure sitting against the wall.

'Flynn?'

No answer.

'Flynn?' I take a step closer and nudge the figure with my foot.

'Yep?' His voice startles me. He sounds matter-of-fact, conversational even, as if it is perfectly normal to be sitting here, alone in the dark.

'What are you doing? Everyone's asking where you are.'

'Oh, right.'

I wait. He doesn't move. I can make out the contours of his face. His eyes are bright in the darkness.

'Was this a stupid idea?' I ask quietly.

Flynn suddenly stands up and takes my hand. 'I love you,' he whispers. 'Let's get out of here.'

'What?' I say stupidly. I don't know which throws me

more – Flynn telling me he loves me, or his suggestion that we ditch the party we are hosting. 'What are you talking about? We can't just walk out!'

'Yes we can,' Flynn answers. 'The fire escape. Everyone else is too wasted to even notice.'

'But . . .' I wish I could clear my head and find a suitable reply. Even in my less-than-sober state, I know that Flynn's suggestion is ridiculous. But he is already pulling me firmly towards the bedroom window.

'Wait!' I say urgently. 'I haven't got any shoes on.' As if that is the only reason I shouldn't be climbing down a fire escape in the middle of the night.

'You can have mine,' Flynn replies. 'Let's just get out of here first.' He heaves up the sash window and a blast of cold night air hits me in the face.

'This is crazy, Flynn. I've had too much to drink, I might fall,' I protest, but he has already clambered out onto the narrow metal ledge.

'I've got you. Come on, climb out. It's perfectly safe.' His arms are around me. I find myself swinging a leg over the windowsill. My stockinged foot meets with cold, wet metal. 'Eek, it's freezing!'

Flynn has one arm around my waist, the other on the narrow rail that flanks the spiral steps dropping down into the street below. We begin our slow backwards descent. I hold onto each step as I climb down. Even tipsy, I'm aware that if one of us slips on the wet metal, it could be bad. By the time we reach the pavement I am shivering hard. Flynn takes off his trainers and I step into them. They're warm. I start to laugh. We are standing under the orange glow of the streetlamps – me in my strappy black cocktail dress with a pair of enormous blue and white trainers on my feet, Flynn in his jeans and holey socks. He takes off the suede jacket I gave him for his birthday and puts it round me. I push my arms into it gratefully. Then he grabs me by the hand and breaks into a jog. I clump behind him in the oversized trainers, panting and laughing into the cold night air. 'Where are we going?' I gasp. 'This is so bad – I left Ellen to light the candles on the cake, everyone's going to be looking for us . . .'

We are heading across the busy main road, pausing in the middle to try and dodge the traffic. A taxi takes pity on us and flashes its lights to let us past. As soon as we reach the pavement we break into a run towards the open gates of the park.

'Flynn, ow – ow – I've got a stitch.' I dig my fist into my side and bend double, still being pulled along relentlessly. The slap of my feet against the footpath slows as we leave the bright lights of the high street behind us. Tall trees reach up towards a velvet sky sprinkled with stars. Flynn drags me up a small hill and down the other side, towards the lake. Finally we come to a halt, and I collapse face down on the wet, cold grass.

After several minutes of desperate gasping, the pounding in my head begins to recede and my lungs cease to cry out for air. I lift my face from the damp-smelling earth and prop myself up on my elbows, looking across at a large shimmering expanse of water, silver in the moonlight. The swans look ghostly, gliding effortlessly by.

Flynn has walked down to the water's edge and is standing, hands in pockets, gazing out. I watch him for a moment or two but he is completely still. I pull myself up to a kneeling position and button the jacket around me.

'Flynn?' I say.

He doesn't move.

'Flynn?' I stand up slowly and walk towards him. At the rim of the lake I take his hand and lean against him.

'Isn't this better than a room full of people?' He looks at me, his eyes bright.

'I suppose.' I pull his arm around me. 'But colder.' I look down at his feet and start to laugh. 'God, look at your socks, they're soaked!'

He ignores me and leans forwards and his mouth meets mine. I teeter for a moment and try and pull him back, away from the water's edge. 'Careful,' I say.

He refuses to move back and tries to kiss me again.

'If you fall in, don't think I'm going to rescue you,' I warn. I pull him back towards me and we sit down on the grass. 'Happy birthday, by the way.'

He looks at me and smiles. My heart does a funny fluttering thing in my chest. Even though it's been over two years, it still feels so strange that we are together. I have known Flynn since we were eleven, ever since I met him and Harry at music camp and we started hanging around as a threesome. I've fancied him for years. Apparently he's fancied me for years. But it took us a long time to get together.

'Thank you for the party,' Flynn whispers in my ear.

I start to laugh. 'Yes, well, I can see that you enjoyed it.'

He laughs too. Then kisses me again, so hard I can feel my teeth digging into my lip. He pushes me backwards. I wrap my arms around him and look up at the stars. I wonder if it's possible to explode with happiness.

He is kissing my neck with a familiar urgency. I ruffle his hair and wriggle under the weight of his body. 'Ouch, your keys are cutting into my leg!'

He props himself up on one elbow and digs the bunch of keys out of his jeans pocket, tossing them away onto the grass. His mouth descends back over mine. He kisses me harder, his fingers in my hair. I close my eyes but a sudden sharp pain from the side of my head forces them open again. 'Ow – ow – Flynn, my hair . . .'

He tries to disentangle the offending strand from the clasp of his watch. His face is flushed, his breathing laboured. I screw up my eyes in pain as I feel several hairs being ripped straight out of my head.

'Oh God, it's really hurting!'

'I'm trying!' Flynn exclaims. He snaps open the clasp of his watch, pulls it off his wrist and disengages the last remaining hairs. The watch slips from his fingers and smacks me on the forehead. 'Ouch!' I yell.

'Sorry, sorry . . .' He tosses the watch into the grass

and lowers his face back to mine. I taste his lips, his mouth, his tongue . . . There is something digging into my back, just against my spine. I try to ignore it. Flynn shifts against me and the pain intensifies. It feels like a twig – a twig with a knobbly bit sticking out, jabbing into my bone . . . Maybe it's not even a twig, maybe it's a piece of glass—

'For heaven's sake, what is it now?' Flynn shouts as I wince with pain.

'I'm lying on something – just get off me for one second . . .'

Flynn pulls himself up to a kneeling position, breathing hard. 'I swear to God, Jennah, if you think this is funny . . .'

'I don't, I don't!' I sit up and feel behind me in the grass. 'Look, it was a stone! Look how sharp—'

Flynn tries to pull me back down onto the grass, but there is a rustling sound coming from the path behind us. I pull away and hold my breath. Between the trees I can make out the figure of a late-night jogger. I motion to Flynn to be quiet. He heaves a loud sigh and drops back onto the ground with his arms spread out. I watch the man continue along the path, around the curve of the pond and over the grass towards the gate. I look down at Flynn. He has his eyes closed.

I start to laugh. 'I don't really think I'm the outdoorsy type.'

He opens his eyes and sits up. 'What about being adventurous and spontaneous?'

I laugh and lean back on my hands, resting my head against his shoulder. 'I'm sorry.' I start to giggle again.

He glares down at me. 'You are *so* not forgiven.'

I inhale deeply and look up at the night sky. 'Oh, look at the moon!'

It is round and full, a large cardboard cut-out hanging low in the sky. 'Make a birthday wish,' I say.

Flynn closes his eyes. There is a silence. Then he opens them.

'Done?' I ask.

'Done,' he says.

'What was it?'

He glances at me. 'Can't tell you or it won't come true.'

'Oh please!' I say. 'Please, just one tiny clue?'

He looks at me and smiles. 'Something about you.'

Chapter Two

FLYNN

I teeter on the edge of wakefulness, the pink glow behind my closed eyelids suggesting it is already late morning. Voices drift up from the street below and I find myself gliding effortlessly into a meadow as sleep takes me again, spiriting me along, weightless as a breeze. The voices take on the form of two old men sitting on a bench in the middle of a forest, and I brush the tops of their felt hats as I pass, and then I feel myself rising up, towards the dappled sunlight falling between the leaves. The trees are hundreds of metres high and the sun is nothing but a shimmering corner of distant gold. I'm rising, rising, reaching out, trying to touch the tops of the trees and the clear blue sky that I know lies above. I wake.

The room is flooded with sunlight, slanting in through the partly drawn curtains. Around the bed, remnants of a late night – clothes on the floor, an overflowing laundry basket, a toppled pile of library books, a scattering of hairgrips across the carpet. Beside the window, the desk is piled high with clutter from the living-room table – bills and uni notices and photocopies and lever-arch files. Beside me, her head falling off the pillow, Jennah lies sprawled on her front, her arm hanging off the side of the bed. Her shoulder blades are visible under the thin white T-shirt she sleeps in and a fine golden down covers her bare arms, still tanned from the hot summer. Her long chestnut hair is spread out across the white pillow. I roll onto my side, propping myself up on one elbow to look over at her still-sleeping face. Her lashes are dark against her cheek. I lean over her slowly, carefully, and kiss her forehead. I want to do more but I stop myself, afraid of waking her. I content myself with looking at her instead. I was touched that she went to all that trouble yesterday – once I got over the initial shock of finding our tiny flat crammed full of people. I remember the descent down the fire escape and smile to myself. That was the highlight of my day. Leaving the heaving flat and walking through Hyde Park with Jennah. Kissing her next to the moonlit water. I break my resolve and reach out a hand and stroke her cheek. She sighs and stirs but does not wake. I still can't believe it. Still can't believe she is here, with me, in our flat, in our room, in our bed. Still can't believe she is my girlfriend.

I get up quietly and pad to the bathroom. When I've finished peeing, I pull on some jeans and go into the kitchen to put the coffee on. I fill a tall glass with tap water and take my pills at the sink, looking out over the small back gardens. I put two slices of bread in the toaster and peel and cut up an apple. Hm, apple and toast, not exactly a luxurious breakfast. There are some tinned cherries in the cupboard. I open them and add them to the apple slices. I put some honey on top for good measure. The toast pops up and I spread butter and jam. I make up a bowl of cereal and put the lot onto a chopping board. I carry it back to the bedroom. She is still asleep. I sit cross-legged on the floor, the chopping board on my knees, and look hard at her, willing her to wake. As I watch her sleeping, I feel suddenly frightened – frightened that all this could be taken away. She blinks at me and smiles.

'Morning, you.' She rolls onto her side and stretches. 'What time is it?'

'Twelve.'

She sits up, rubbing her eyes sleepily. 'What are you doing down there?'

'I brought you breakfast.' I carry the chopping board over to the bed.

She kneels up and kisses me as I hand her a mug of coffee. 'Has anyone ever told you you're an angel?'

'Well, it *is* the weekend.'

She smiles down at the chopping board. 'You made fruit salad!' She tucks in while I sip my coffee. She tries to feed me cherries. I decline. I can never eat till the caffeine has kicked in.

'Ah, Sunday,' Jennah says between sips of coffee. 'My favourite day of the week.'

I give a wry smile. 'I take it you've blanked out yesterday then?'

She gives me a look. 'Oh God, is the mess awful?'

I pretend to consider the question for a moment. 'Depends how you define *awful*.'

We get up soon after and attack the living room. Jennah is something of a neatness freak. I am not. But I try. When the last ashtray is emptied and the final rubbish bag carried downstairs, I get stuck into the mountain of washing-up and Jennah does the vacuuming. An hour later and we collapse together into a hot bath.

It is late afternoon before I get down to any serious practice. Jennah has an essay to do for her Psychology of Performance module so I use the keyboard and headphones. I am halfway through my third hour when my brother comes by to take me out to supper. Jennah won't come because her essay is overdue.

'So how are things?' Rami asks as our food arrives. We are in a pizzeria, sitting at a small table next to the window overlooking the street. 'Have lectures started up again yet?'

'Yeah, we've got a shitty timetable this year,' I reply. 'We don't even have Fridays off any more.'

'My heart bleeds,' Rami says. 'And I bet the ten o'clock lectures are a real shock to the system after the three months' holiday.'

I take a gulp of Coke and shoot my brother a look. 'Finals are only eight months away. I don't remember you being so glib when you were cramming for your medical exams.'

'Oh right, and I suppose a sound knowledge of the

human anatomy and embryological development is the same as listening to a piece of music and saying how it makes you feel—'

I take a swipe at Rami's head. 'Fuck off.'

Rami grins. 'Sorry I couldn't make it yesterday. There just wasn't anyone to cover my shift.'

Rami and his wife Sophie are doctors at the same hospital and often work at weekends.

'Sounds like you all had a cool time. Did you really not see it coming?'

I shake my head. 'Jennah seemed a bit on edge in the morning but I thought she was just having an essay crisis.'

'How are things going with you two?'

'Fine,' I reply guardedly. I tend to be reluctant to discuss the subject of my love-life with my older brother, who, being twelve years my senior and happily married with a baby daughter, feels it his duty to dole out barrels of unwanted advice.

'I know it's only been a couple of months, but do you think it's working out, the two of you living together?'

'Yes.' I nod vigorously, unable to hide my enthusiasm. Rami starts to smile.

'What?' I demand, my cheeks hot.

'You have that look.'

'What look?'

Rami is grinning. 'The loved-up look. And now you're going red.'

'Fuck off!' I say again loudly. The waitress turns in surprise.

I press my fists to my cheeks and lower my voice. 'So how's work?'

'Uh-uh. You're not getting off that lightly,' Rami protests. 'How are you finding it, living with a woman? Bet you're having to shower on a slightly more regular basis!'

I kick him under the table but laugh despite myself.

Rami picks up his glass. 'Well, cheers. Happy birthday.'

I smile. 'I think it's going to be a good year.'

Harry is seated at the kitchen table when I arrive back at the flat. Jennah is at the counter, making coffee. Harry is my closest and oldest friend. We shared a flat together during our first three years at the Royal College of Music. We are opposites in every way. He is a beanpole with black corkscrew curls and a permanent look of amusement on his face. Despite being a talented cellist, he has his feet firmly on the ground and is essentially conformist. He is a good guy though. I see less of him now that Jennah and I are living together – the dynamics of the group have changed since we used to hang around as a threesome – and of course there is his relationship with Kate.

'Hey, it's the birthday boy!' He gets up and slaps an arm round my shoulders.

'Not till Tuesday actually. How's it going?'

'Crap,' Harry says bluntly. 'I've got an essay for tomorrow.'

I laugh. Harry is renowned for making heavy weather of essays.

'Coffee, Flynn?' Jennah asks me.

'It's all right, I'll make it.'

Jennah takes a cup off the rack. 'It's already made.'

I sit down at the kitchen table opposite Harry. 'Did you have fun last night?' I ask him.

'It was a good night,' Harry replied. 'And I can't believe you two have got this place looking spotless so soon after. Talk about nesting instincts . . .'

I flick a grape across at Harry's head. 'Shut it!'

'And where the hell did you disappear to, anyway?' Harry wants to know. 'Ellen ended up blowing out the candles herself.'

Jennah's gaze meets mine and I try not to smile.

Harry notices. His eyes widen with a look of amused horror. 'Don't tell me you were . . . Oh no, you weren't—'

'It's not what you're thinking!' Jennah squawks, turning pink. 'My God, you men only have one thing on the brain! We went for a walk in the park!'

'Well, we didn't exactly do very much walking,' I interject, determined to wind her up.

Harry begins to laugh.

Jennah gasps in outrage. 'We sat and watched the swans on the lake, thank you very much, Harry!'

Harry is still laughing. 'Now could that possibly be a euphemism for—'

Jennah yelps and whacks Harry on the back of the

head. Harry cries out in mock outrage. 'Aargh! Is this how she treats you, Flynn? Whacking you if you don't make the bed in the morning, whacking you if you don't put the loo seat down—!'

Jennah pretends to throttle him. I laugh.

We spend the rest of the evening together. Jennah is meant to be helping Harry with his essay but not a lot of work gets done. She uncorks a bottle of wine and we end up playing a rather drunken game of What's That Tune? Harry provokes no end of hilarity when it transpires he can't sing when pissed.

'Listen! Listen!' Harry is shouting, bouncing up and down on the sofa in annoyance. He tries the song again, a lengthy string of *na-na-na-nas*, accompanied by some rhythm-less drumming on the coffee table.

'Theme tune from *Lord of the Rings*!' I shout. 'No, *Star Wars, Star Wars*!'

'Stop doing action films!' Jennah wails. 'That's not fair, I told you—'

'*Listen!*' Harry yells, drowning out our protests. '*Na-na-na-na-na-na-na-na-na!*' He karate-chops the coffee table for emphasis.

'Oh my God, it isn't even a tune!' Jennah yells. 'I know, it's rap! It's a rapper! Eminem!'

'Are you tone deaf or what?' Harry yells at her. 'Of course it's got a tune! It's in F minor, you idiot! *Na-na-na-na-na . . .*'

'Couldn't you at least choose a different syllable?' I beg.

'I'll give you a clue,' Harry offers generously. 'Something to do with strawberries and cream.'

'I know! I know!' Jennah dives off the end of the couch, sprawling at Harry's feet. 'The Wimbledon tune!'

'Ta-da!' Harry declares, holding out his arms.

'No way!' I roar. '*Na-na-na-na* is the Wimbledon tune?'

'It's not the kind of thing you can really sing.' Harry is defensive.

'The Wimbledon tune sounds nothing like that!' I yell, jumping to my feet. 'That's crap! The Wimbledon tune is completely different! It goes like . . .' I hesitate, trying to think.

Harry explodes with a triumphant guffaw. 'You see! You can't sing it either!'

'I've got it, I've got it!' I *la* a few bars.

'That's what I said!' Harry yells.

We don't get to bed until three in the morning, by which time Harry has passed out on the couch. I sleep lightly and wake at dawn. I have noticed that I need less and less sleep lately, which pleases me. Since being diagnosed with bipolar disorder two and a half years ago, I have been taking a mood-stabilizer, a drug called lithium, which is supposed to iron out my moods. It does the trick – stops me from swinging between being hyper and awake all night, to depressed and unable to get out of bed. But the side-effects – feeling sluggish and often queasy – are a right pain. Recently, however, I seem to be getting some of my old energy back, and I'm delighted. The Royal College of Music is a pressure-cooker environment at the best of times, filled with aspiring young musicians dreaming of stardom and prepared to make a hell of a lot of sacrifices to get there. You need to be on top form just to survive, just to keep up with the rest, let alone get ahead. And if you want to stand a chance of making it as a professional musician in the big wide world, you *have* to get ahead, even while still at uni. You have to find a way of rising above the rest, of sticking out from the crowd. And the only way to do that is to practise, practise, practise, and then go out and win a hell of a lot of competitions. I have won three international competitions this year and I've already received a handful of concert bookings for after I graduate. But it's not enough. It's never enough.

I drink some coffee and make the most of my early morning by donning my headphones and grinding through twenty pages of Czerny at my keyboard. Harry rolls off the couch just before nine, downs a coffee and some aspirin before heading to lectures, still looking half asleep. I remember I have an essay to write for my Aesthetics and Criticism class but push it to the back of my mind for now. One lesson I have learned from my cognitive therapy sessions with Dr Stefan is to compartmentalize – to arrange the different parts of my life like pigeon-holes in my brain and only focus on one compartment at a time. It's supposed to stop you from feeling overloaded, although the hundreds of pigeon-holes I see whenever I try this technique still manage to freak me out every time.

Jennah makes me jump with a kiss and a cup of coffee sometime after ten. I pull my headphones down round my neck and keep on playing arpeggios with one hand, taking the cup with the other. Jennah puts her arms around me and nuzzles my ear as I continue to play one-handed.

'Harry took off about half an hour ago,' I inform her.

'I'm not surprised, with you thudding away. How long have you been at it?'

'Couple of hours.' It's easier to lie. For some reason Jennah gets nervous if I practise too much. She is wearing her white bathrobe and her hair is wet and smells of apricot shampoo. I put my coffee down on the end of the keyboard and go back to my arpeggios, headphones still round my neck. I have the sound on so high, I can still just about hear what I am playing. Jennah comes round and perches on my knee. I put my arm round her so that I can reach the bottom octave.

'Flynn?' She kisses my face.

'Mm.'

'Have you got lectures this morning?'

'Mm.'

'Come and have breakfast with me?'

'Mm.'

She presses her nose against mine, completely obscuring my view of the keyboard. I find myself staring into her large dark green eyes. Her irises are flecked with gold. I keep playing.

'Wrong note!' she cries, triumphant.

'No!' I protest.

'Liar.'

I laugh.

'I'm so hungry I could eat you,' she says.

'OK, OK!' I reach behind her and turn off the keyboard. 'Talk about distracting!'

'You know what they say about concert pianists,' she says, dragging me to the kitchen.

'What's that then?'

She puts the toast on. 'Can't be a top concert pianist if you're in love.' She twirls around, her bathrobe flapping against the fridge door.

'Huh. Well, who said I was in love?'

'Bastard!' she gasps dramatically in mock outrage.

I laugh and kiss her.

The Royal College is a university that never sleeps. From early in the morning till late at night, the marble entrance hall resonates with the strains of some instrument. On the steps outside, students come and go, carrying scores and music books and large black instrument cases. On the first floor, the wood-panelled lecture hall is filled with sleeping students as Professor Meyers mumbles his way through a mind-numbing lecture on the rise of expressive monody in the late sixteenth century. On the bench next to me, Harry has given up his doodling and looks to be sound asleep, his glasses askew. I practise the fingering to Rachmaninov's Second Piano Concerto on the edge of the desk and think about Jennah, the concerto, Professor Kaiser, my essay on the role and development of incidental music in nineteenth-century stage productions . . . My mind is jumping about all over the place this morning. It's a feeling I've missed.

Jennah has rehearsals for the Christmas concert all through her lunch break, but I've promised to deliver her a sandwich. Music explodes from the double doors that lead to the concert hall. Mozart's *Laudate Dominum* – a piece Jennah has been practising for weeks. I sneak in through the swing doors at the back of the amphitheatre, holding the sandwich out of view of Professor Williams, who is leading the rehearsals, and take a seat near the back. Jennah and the other two soloists are sitting on the edge of the concert platform, looking bored, while Williams talks to the first violinist about quarter rests. Jennah says something to the girl sitting next to her, laughs, and earns herself an angry '*Shh!*' from Williams. She sighs, then yawns and starts pulling the loose threads off the bottom of her long denim skirt. She hasn't seen me.

Williams is clapping his hands together, trying to get people's attention. By now, everyone has begun to talk, and the murmurs rise like the buzz from a beehive. 'A bit of quiet, please!' he bellows, waving his baton like a wand. I am so glad I'm not involved in the concert this term. Williams goes over to the piano and plays an A. The sound of tuning is deafening. Finally there is silence. Williams draws himself up self-importantly and raises his baton. Then he looks at Jennah. She is trying to fix the broken zip on her ankle boots. Someone nudges her.

'First soloist!' Williams barks.

Jennah pulls a face and stands quickly, brushing the hair out of her eyes. Williams gives her a long look, then drops his baton. The music begins . . .

When Jennah starts to sing, I feel the goose pimples rise on my arms. I haven't heard her sing this piece with the orchestra before. Her voice is strong and pure, resonating through the hall. She sways forward onto her toes and gazes out to the back of the concert hall, her eyes bright. The sleeves of her grey jumper are too long so I am sure I am the only one to notice when she taps her finger against her skirt to help her with a re-entry. I can almost taste her voice in my mouth. It is the colour of dawn. I want to run up and grab her and twirl her around. I want to yell, *She's mine!* The sight of her, standing there, singing, makes me want to shout with joy.

Chapter Three

JENNAH

Flynn arrived in time to hear me sing *Laudate Dominum*, which pleased me no end. I'd been watching the double doors for most of the lunchtime rehearsal, hoping he would get here before it was my turn to sing. When he finally snuck in, holding the sandwich he'd promised me, I looked away quickly and pretended I hadn't seen him. I don't know why exactly – I suppose I didn't want him to realize I was waiting for him. It also reduced the risk of eye-contact when I got up to sing. And it meant that I could be secretly aware of *him* watching *me*, which is always fun. When Professor Williams finally gave us a break, Flynn came over to the platform and handed me my sandwich. We chatted for a few minutes but he didn't really hang around for long because the two other soloists were with us, and Flynn is funny around people he doesn't know.

This evening, Harry comes round to work on the Aesthetics and Criticism essay we both have to write. Flynn has an evening lesson with Professor Kaiser, the infamous German piano maestro at the Royal College.

The lesson is only meant to last an hour but usually runs into two or three and so I am glad to have Harry to spend the evening with. Unlike Flynn, I don't do the solitary thing too well. And Harry is like the brother I never had. I put on the pasta while he sits at the kitchen table and sifts through the hundreds of scrawled notes I seem to have amassed.

'You've got enough for three essays here, Jen.'

'Yes, but most of it is probably irrelevant. You know how Professor Meyers likes to drone on and on.' I join him at the table and we get to work, passing books and notes back and forth, occasionally reading a sentence aloud to each other to see how it sounds. Harry types his essay straight onto his laptop while I scribble it all out onto pages and pages of lined paper. The stove makes a loud sizzling sound as the water boils over. I drain the pasta, shake a bottle of sauce into it, and Harry and I each take a fork and eat it straight out of the saucepan. Cooking has never been my strong point. After a couple more hours of academic drudgery I make some coffee. I have only managed a thousand words and Harry even less. The essay is due in at nine a.m. tomorrow. Looks like it's going to be a long night.

Sometime around ten, Flynn comes in, cheeks pink from the night air, hair damp from the rain.

'How was the lesson?' I ask him.

'Great!' He kisses me hard, his hand freezing against my face. His mouth tastes of beer.

'Have you been to the pub?' I ask in surprise.

'Yeah! Met up with André and Bertie. André came second in the Chopin competition. Wanted to drown his sorrows.'

'Why didn't *you* enter the Chopin competition?' Harry asks.

'Don't like Chopin.' Flynn throws open the fridge and begins scavenging for food. 'Are you two still working on that essay? You're so boring.' He takes out some eggs and starts making himself an omelette, still wearing his coat. He puts the bowl on top of my pile of papers and starts greasing the pan right next to Harry's laptop. 'Why don't you just write the same essay? One of you could write the first half and the other could write the second half.'

'I think Meyers might notice if we hand in two identical essays,' Harry says drily, leafing through *An Anatomy of Musical Criticism.* I start rewriting a clumsy sentence for the fourth time.

'They'd hardly be identical! Not with all your spelling mistakes!' Flynn starts to laugh.

I look up at Flynn in surprise. Harry is mildly dyslexic, and although it has never been a big deal, I have never heard Flynn make a joke of it before. Harry just shakes his head good-naturedly and moves his laptop out of harm's way as Flynn starts to grate cheese energetically onto a plate. Soon, more than the plate is covered. I pick bits of cheese off the open pages of the library books. 'Couldn't you do that on the counter?'

As Flynn starts whisking the eggs, we move over to the

living room to grind on with our essays. Flynn joins us to eat his omelette but turns on the television so loud we have to ask him to turn it down. He seems restless, practising at the keyboard, then vacuuming the flat, finally climbing onto the back of the sofa, bouncing a tennis ball annoyingly over our heads against the opposite wall. It is an effort to stop myself from snapping.

'What was that quote from *Authenticity and Early Music*?' Harry asks me as the tennis ball thuds against the wall behind us. 'Something about the critical issues raised by period instruments . . . I wrote it down somewhere and now I've lost it . . .' He shifts wearily through a pile of papers.

I try to find the page for him in the relevant book. 'The one about authentic texts?'

'No, it was in the other book, the Kenyon one. Something about period instruments . . .'

I lift up books and papers from the coffee table, trying to find the elusive book. 'Where's it gone? I had it just a second ago. I'm so tired I'm seeing double. Isn't that the Kenyon book, behind your—' I break off as the tennis ball hits me squarely on the back of the head.

'Jesus, Flynn!'

There's a silence. I have startled myself with the force of my shout. Harry pulls an embarrassed face and looks down at his laptop. Flynn jumps down from the back of the sofa and treads all over my notes, looking for his ball. I grab it and hold it behind my back. He lunges at me.

'Children, please . . .' Harry tries to add some humour to the situation.

Flynn grabs my arm. 'Give me back my ball.'

'No!' I shout.

'Give it back!'

'No!'

'Why?'

'You're driving us crazy, that's why! Can't you see we're trying to write this essay? We've got exactly eight hours before it has to be handed in! You can either help us with it or go to bed!'

Flynn only grunts in reply, still trying to wrestle the ball out of my hand.

'Now, kiddies, come on,' Harry says.

Flynn wins the struggle and whoops in triumph, shooting the ball across to the opposite wall, knocking a picture frame off the mantelpiece.

'For God's sake!' I yell, furious now.

Harry stands up and picks up his laptop. 'Let's go back to the kitchen and leave Flynn to his game of squash,' he suggests calmly. I follow suit, gathering up books and papers. As I follow Harry into the kitchen, there is a crash behind us and the sound of broken glass.

We finally finish our essays at half past four in the morning. I am so tired I can hardly speak. But Harry is worried about Flynn. He seems to think he is getting manic again. I remind him that Flynn's always irritating when he's drunk. I give my essay to Harry to take in and watch him get into his car before stumbling into the bedroom and pulling off my clothes. Flynn has passed out, fully dressed, sprawled across the bed. I shove him unceremoniously off my side and crawl under the duvet. Sleep. At last.

I'm awoken by a rustle and the tread of footsteps across the bedroom floor, followed by the clatter of keys meeting with the surface of the wooden desk. I emerge slowly from the covers, groggy and blurry-eyed, as Flynn throws open the curtains, flooding me with harsh white sunlight.

'Ugh . . .' I groan. 'What time is it?'

'Nearly nine,' he replies. He is wearing his suede jacket with the collar turned up and his cheeks are bright pink. 'You don't have lectures this morning, do you?'

'What day is it?'

'Tuesday.'

'I have Professional Skills at eleven.' I yawn. 'And don't you have Conducting?'

'Skipped it.' Flynn throws himself across the bed, propping his head up on his hand. 'It's such a beautiful day. Let's go for a walk in the countryside.'

I smile. Out of the two of us, Flynn is definitely the more romantic. I brush the hair out of my face and lean forward to kiss him. His face is pink and cold. 'Where have you been?'

'I needed to buy some stuff from Boots but it wasn't open yet. Do you want breakfast in bed?'

'I think I can make it to the kitchen.' I smile. 'God, you were annoying when you were drunk last night.'

'I wasn't drunk!'

'Yeah, right,' I say disbelievingly.

He kisses me again. 'I'll make it up to you. Let's skip uni today and go to Chessington.'

'An amusement park?' I roll my eyes. 'Aren't we a bit old for that?'

'Then let's go to the river and catch a boat down the Thames. Or go on the London Eye! I know, I know, I'll borrow Harry's car and we can drive down to the coast!'

I laugh at his enthusiasm. Sometimes Flynn reminds me of an overexcited puppy. I feel almost guilty at having to dampen his fireworks.

'Flynn, there's no way I can miss my Aesthetics tutorial. I have to read out my essay today and I've been working on it half the night. Let's save it for the weekend, OK? I'm going to have a shower.'

I drag myself out of bed and go to the bathroom, pulling off my T-shirt. I step into the cold tub and draw the curtain. I turn the shower on full force—

'Jesus!' I am knocked off balance and narrowly miss banging my head on the tiles as Flynn suddenly springs into the bath with me, sending the shower head flying out of my hand. It falls to the bottom of the bath, spurting up a fountain of water into our eyes. 'You nearly gave me a heart attack! What on earth are you doing? Did you even ask me if I wanted—?'

He shuts me up with a kiss . . .

* * *

After my morning lecture I head over to Harry's flat in Bayswater. The flat actually belongs to Harry's parents, who now live in Brussels. Since moving in with Harry last summer, Kate, his girlfriend, has had plans to strip the flat of its austere burgundy wallpaper and paint the walls a pale beige. However, after putting in more than a few weeks worth of elbow-grease over the holidays, she seems to have finally realized she has bitten off more than she can chew. Since term started the flat has been a building site of stripped walls and sheet-clad furniture. The news that Harry's parents were coming over to visit at the end of the month understandably sent Kate into a frenzy, and so in a fit of mad generosity I offered to help her finish decorating.

I find her in paint-stained clothes, smoking a cigarette out of the living-room window, looking harassed. 'Harry helped me finish the kitchen this morning but we've still got the living room and the two bedrooms to do,' she tells me. 'And I think I'm suffering from toxic fumes inhalation.'

'Nothing that a good old-fashioned fag won't put right,' I tease her.

She shoots me a grin, tosses me an old shirt of Harry's and we get to work – Kate applying a second coat of glossy white to the living-room door while I attack the tricky bit around the fireplace. We chat about uni, careers and our respective boyfriends as the afternoon sunlight streams in through the curtainless windows.

At around two, Harry bursts in brandishing pizza and seems suitably impressed by our morning's efforts. I have pains in my legs, back and neck. Kate and I drop our paintbrushes and join him as he rummages around in the kitchen under paint-stained sheets for plates and cutlery. Kate pulls the sheet off the kitchen table and I collapse gratefully onto a stool, comfortably exhausted.

'Who wants coffee?' Harry asks.

'Have you got tea?' I ask.

'No, but I can ask your other half to pick some up on the way.'

'Flynn's coming over?' I ask in surprise.

'Yeah, I caught him on my way out of uni – he was just finishing off something for Kaiser. Told him to come over and have some pizza with us.' Harry digs his mobile out of his pocket and flicks it open.

'You tricked him into giving us a hand with the painting more like!' Kate laughs.

'Hi, where are you?' Harry speaks into the phone. 'Can you pick up some Earl Grey on your way past the supermarket? Cheers. See you in a bit.' He snaps the mobile shut and returns it to his pocket.

'Where is he?' I ask Harry.

'He's having lunch with a crowd from Music and Literature,' Harry replies, his eyebrows arched in surprise. 'He's becoming very sociable all of a sudden!'

After we've finished gorging ourselves on pizza, we get back to work again. Harry and Kate bicker amicably about the merits of paintbrushes over rollers. Harry gets paint on the cuff of his new shirt and then spends an inordinate length of time trying to get the stain out with white spirit and a nailbrush. Kate points out that if Harry spent more time putting paint on the walls and less time putting paint on himself, there would be a chance his parents wouldn't have to stay in a hotel. Harry points out that he wasn't the one allergic to red wallpaper. Kate points out that she wasn't the one who suggested they move in together. Harry adds that he wasn't the one who used to complain about the long walk home. Kate retorts that she wasn't the one to start this relationship.

'You see what I have to put up with?' Harry turns to me for support.

'Hey.' I hold up my hands, laughing. 'I'm keeping right out of this.'

The buzzer goes and Harry gets up. I sit back on my heels and survey the room. 'We've nearly finished!' I exclaim with satisfaction.

Harry comes back in with Flynn. I stand up for a kiss but Flynn is too busy looking around at the freshly painted walls. 'What colour d'you call this?' he exclaims. 'Vomit?'

'Flynn!' I give him a meaningful look but he doesn't appear to notice. Kate is worried enough already about Harry's parents' reaction.

'Did you remember the tea?' Harry asks him.

'What tea?'

I roll my eyes.

Harry and Flynn go next door to make more coffee. I squat down and pick up my paintbrush again.

'Is it really the colour of vomit?' Kate asks in a small voice.

'No!' I exclaim vehemently. 'It's a lovely soft beige. Flynn just thinks he's being funny.' I can hear the other two in the kitchen. Flynn is talking rapid-fire about some television programme. They come back in, Harry holding coffee mugs, Flynn still talking: '. . . and so you can use the transfer of learning method to practise the same trick with the other hand. Except you don't actually have to use the other hand, so basically you could just practise all day with your right hand and then the next day find that your left hand has learned the sequence of movements without doing any practice at all . . .'

'I thought you said the documentary was about circus clowns learning to juggle,' Harry says, handing out the mugs. 'I don't see how learning to juggle has anything to do with playing the piano—'

'No, I'm talking about the transfer of learning!' Flynn practically shouts. 'Jugglers practise a skill with one hand only and then find that the skill has automatically been transferred by the brain to the other hand! So it means they can cut their practice time in half by training one hand to do one set of skills and then the other hand to do a completely different set of skills, rather than have to repeat the same skills with each hand . . .'

'Who's learning to juggle?' Kate asks with an amused grin.

'Flynn, apparently,' Harry replies with a roll of the eyes.

'This means I could practise harmonic scales with my left hand and dominant scales with my right hand and then my brain would transfer what my right hand had learned to my left hand . . .'

I feel uneasy suddenly. Flynn has a sharp, almost agitated look in his eyes. 'Watch out!' I shout.

Too late. Flynn leans the whole of his left side against the wall that Kate has just finished painting. Kate and I look at each other in horror. Flynn straightens up and peels his arm away from the wet wall, gazing down at the mess of beige paint on his jacket and jeans.

'Whoops.' Harry looks as if he is trying not to laugh.

I look at Flynn's suede jacket and the massive splodge on the wet wall with bits of fluff stuck to it. 'Anyway,' Flynn goes on, taking off his jacket and tossing it onto the floor – apparently unaware that it's now ruined – 'I'm going to put it into practice by learning a fast new piece with my right hand and then the next day I'll see if I can do it with my left hand, and I should get exactly the same results, because if it works with juggling—'

'Flynn, stop talking for a sec,' I cut in, worry making my voice sound harsh. 'Why don't you sit down and have something to eat?'

But now he is off again about how juggling is going

to make a significant difference to his practice schedule. Harry and Kate, good-natured as usual, seem to be finding it all quite amusing.

'I'm sure Professor Kaiser will be delighted when you inform him you've given up the Rach Two in favour of one-handed juggling.' Harry laughs. 'Just let me know in advance so I can watch the spectacle from a distance.'

'You don't believe me. I'll show you.' Flynn downs his coffee in three loud gulps and jumps up.

'Jesus,' Harry breathes. 'How does that not burn your mouth?'

Flynn whisks the sheet off the desk like a magician, uncovering Kate's computer and a plethora of office knick-knacks.

'Hey, careful, I mustn't get paint on that—' Kate begins.

'OK, now, watch!' Ignoring her, Flynn grabs a stapler, a roll of sellotape and the remote control, throws them in the air and attempts to juggle. Kate yelps as the stapler hits her on the arm.

'Hold on, hold on, this really isn't the best room for a circus act . . .' Harry protests, his laughter fading slightly.

'The walls are wet!' Kate says desperately as Flynn grabs the offending articles off the floor and tries again.

'Watch, watch! I've been practising and it isn't actually that difficult!'

'Flynn, this isn't funny!' I yell. The stapler, sellotape and remote go skidding across the floor again and this time I get to them first. Flynn is momentarily distracted by a large tub of paint by the door and drags it to the centre of the room. 'Hey, I know how we can get rid of this vomit paint! Have any of you heard of the artist Chris Ofili?' His voice is so loud, he is almost shouting. I am starting to feel frightened.

'Flynn, that's the paint for the front door . . .' Kate looks frantic.

'You remember him, don't you, Jen?' Flynn continues as if she hasn't spoken. 'We saw some of his exhibits last year at the Tate Modern.' He squats down in front of the paint bucket and begins to prise the lid open with his fingertips. 'He was the guy who did the Virgin Mary out of elephant shit and won the Turner Prize—'

'Flynn, that's black paint!' I shout. Then several things happen at once. The lid flies off and Flynn plunges the paintbrush into the inky pool. Kate's hand shoots out to stop him and knocks over Harry's coffee. Harry jumps to his feet and tries to grab Flynn's arm. Flynn jumps back, dodging him easily, and shakes the paint-loaded brush vigorously, sending a splattering of black drops onto the nearest wall.

Kate lets out a small scream.

'What the hell are you doing?' Harry yells, his eyes wide with disbelief.

'Wait, wait, I haven't finished!' Flynn dodges Harry and dives for the paint tin again. 'Look, it has a speckled effect, you have to do each wall in turn, all you do is shake it like this . . .'

Kate jumps up, looking close to tears, and flees the room. Harry lunges again for Flynn's arm, misses, slips in the spilled coffee and crashes to the floor. Flynn starts to laugh. 'Yeah, this is what I'm talking about! Abstract art – scene of a struggle – get paint and put it on your clothes, press yourself to the wall, the paint will show the movements of your body, like shadows, like spectres . . .' He dips his hands into the black paint and slaps them against the freshly painted wall, smearing black streaks into the wet beige.

'What are you doing?' Harry tries to block him but Flynn just grabs Harry by the shoulders and pushes him back against the wet wall.

'Stand still!' Flynn shouts. 'I'm going to paint round you! Now this is how you create a shadow . . .'

Harry attempts another desperate lunge for Flynn's arm and Flynn grabs a handful of paint and smears it onto Harry's clothes. Harry tries to wrestle Flynn to the floor, but with the speed of lightning, Flynn escapes Harry's grasp. I realize I haven't moved since the carnage began. It's as if my body has gone into shock and all my muscles have frozen. I force myself forward, towards Flynn, who is now smearing handfuls of black paint down his own sleeves, over his jeans . . .

'Oh my God, he's lost it, this time he's really lost it . . .' Harry stares in horror, starting to back away.

'Flynn, stop it!' My voice shakes, and I try to grab his hands. 'Stop it! Look what you're doing! You're destroying Harry's flat!'

Flynn laughs. 'I know, I know, I know, it looks great – d'you wanna help? Look, Jen, you just have to put it on your hands and then press your hands to the wall and then—'

I've got hold of one arm, Harry grabs hold of the other. Flynn shoves us off him, hard, and overturns the tin of paint.

'Ha ha ha! You wanna play catch? You think you can get me? You think you can catch me?' He leaps effortlessly up onto the table. I grab the tail of Flynn's shirt and hang on for dear life. Flynn drags himself away from me and the shirt rips in my hand. Harry grasps hold of one leg and Flynn kicks him away. Harry staggers backwards, gasping, holding his side. 'I'm calling the police—'

'No! Call an ambulance – just call an ambulance, please, Harry.' I am almost sobbing. Harry staggers from the room. I crawl up onto the table. Grab hold of Flynn's arm and hang on for dear life.

'Flynn stop – please stop – just sit down – Flynn, *please!*' I am clawing at his clothes, trying to drag him down from the table. He pulls away easily, leaps onto the back of the sofa, then starts climbing onto the bookshelves. He pulls out a handful of books and hurls them down into the growing pool of black paint. 'It's art, it's art!' he whoops. 'Can't you see? It's modern art!'

Harry is pulling me back by the arm towards the open door.

'No, Harry,' I protest. 'We've got to—'

'They're coming, the ambulance is on its way.' Harry's grip on my wrist is like iron as he forces me out into the corridor. He closes the living-room door and holds onto the handle.

I try to force my way back in. 'No, Harry, no!' I protest frantically. 'The window – he might jump!'

'He's getting violent!' Harry shouts back. 'We've got to stay out here!'

My knees give way and I sink to the floor. Harry is still hanging onto the door handle. From inside the living room, the crashing continues.

'We've got to try and help him!' I beg.

'Believe me, this is the kindest thing we could do,' Harry says quietly. 'The last thing he'd want would be to hurt you.'

And so he restrains me until the wail of the ambulance rises from the street.

Chapter Four

FLYNN

There are bright lights and busy corridors. Lots of corridors, lots of people. Everyone is tall. The people around me are green. One is pushing this chair, the other is walking. I am gliding along in this magic chair. The speckled lino keeps disappearing under my feet. The ambulance was tiring. Everything is tiring. All these corridors, all these white lights, all these people. The corridors are very long. At the end of each one there is another. And another. And another. And another.

Finally we stop. There are lots of voices but no people. There's a bed. Curtains drawn around me and the bed. The first green man says, 'I better stay with this one till the doc comes round.' The second green man says, 'I'm going to head back. I'll catch up with you later.' The second green man disappears through a gap in the curtains. The first green man sits down on the edge of the bed. I close my eyes.

There is a hand on my arm. A woman in a white coat is sitting opposite me. She has curly hair. 'Hello,' she says. 'I'm Doctor Stanton. Do you know where you are?'

I look at her. I blink.

'What's your name?' she asks.

I look at her some more. I say my name in my head, but no sound comes out. My lips have been glued together.

'You're at the Chelsea and Westminster Hospital,' the woman says. 'You were brought in by ambulance because you'd been acting strangely. You've been given a large dose of sedative, which is why you're finding it difficult to talk right now. But I want you to try. Can you remember what happened?'

Her eyes are green. With little flecks of gold. Just like Jennah's.

'Flynn, open your eyes a minute.' Her voice is very loud. 'Open your eyes. That's it. What's all this black stuff on you? Is it paint? Do you remember the paint?'

Her eyes are like Jennah's. But her face is not. Her face is nothing like Jennah's. Even her hair is different.

'Right,' says the woman. 'The nurses are going to clean you up. Then we'll get you into bed.' She puts a hand under my chin and shines a light into my eyes. My head hurts. Jennah, where are you?

My skin burns. The nurses keep rubbing with foul-smelling liquid and cotton wool. One is doing my hands and my arms. The other is doing my face. My eyes sting. It takes a long time.

They take off my shirt and jeans. They are covered in some kind of black stuff. I have to stand up but my legs aren't working. They make me get into a white bed. The sheets hurt my skin. I am so tired. I want to sleep. But the bed starts to move. Strips of light flash past overhead. More corridors, more people. I close my eyes.

Rami is here. He is talking to a man in a white coat. We are in a long room with lots more beds. People keep coming and going. One man is attached to a bag on a pole. There is the smell of school dinners. Sunlight streams through a wall of windows. There are flowers in vases. Cards. Balloons. Is it my birthday?

Rami is sitting on a chair close to my bed. He is holding a clipboard and reading intently. He looks at me. He smiles but it doesn't reach his eyes. 'Hey, buddy,' he says. He squeezes my arm. I open my mouth. Something warm and wet trickles down my chin. Rami's eyes water and he turns away.

The windows are full of night. The lights are dim. Someone is groaning loudly in the bed opposite me. If I turn my head to the right, I can see into the corridor. There is a big desk. People behind the desk. On the other side there is another long room just like this one. There is somebody crying out, 'Help me, help me.' Help me too. I'm lost and I'm falling.

It's morning. Sunlight streams in through the wall of windows. It's busy; people are walking about with trolleys. There is that food smell again and the clattering of plates and cutlery. I have never needed to pee so badly in my life. But it's an effort just to move.

I sit up slowly and lower my feet to the floor. I'm only wearing a T-shirt and boxers. The floor is cold. My legs are tired. I try to stand up. I wobble. I am walking through thick soup. It's an effort not to fall. Someone touches my arm. 'Where are you going?' they ask. 'Toilet,' I answer. 'Last door on the right,' they say. I keep on walking. I'm not moving very fast.

I reach a door that says TOILET. I go inside. It takes me a very long time to lock the door. I pee for ages. When I've finished, I go back to my bed. I want to lie down.

There is a table over the bed. They want me to eat cereal. I take one mouthful and feel ready to throw up. I lie back down. They pat my arm. They say I have to eat. I ignore them.

A woman in a white coat is standing by my bed. She asks me how I'm feeling. She shines a light in my eyes. She asks me to follow her finger. She asks me lots of questions – my name, my age, the date, the season, where I live, where I am now, why I came to hospital. Sometimes I answer, sometimes I shrug. When she leaves, I close my eyes.

The nurse says I have to get up. She says the psychiatrist is ready to see me now. She takes me down the corridor to a little room. There is a man with a beard who stands up and shakes my hand. He is smartly dressed. He has a badge. I can't read what it says. We sit down on brown chairs. He asks me lots of questions about the bipolar and the lithium. He says I have to take a stronger dose now.

When I return to my bed, Rami and Jennah are there. Jennah looks frightened. There are purple half-moons under her eyes. My heart squeezes. 'Nice to see you a little more vertical, old man,' Rami says. 'I'll be back in a bit.' He winks and walks off. I get into bed and sit up against the headboard.

Jennah is sitting on the plastic chair. She is nervously tucking her hair behind her ears and trying to smile. 'You've still got paint in your hair.'

I look at her. 'Oh.'

She looks away and bites her lip. Her eyes glisten.

I want to touch her but I don't dare. I don't even know if she's mine any more.

'Are you feeling a bit better?' The words catch in her throat but she smiles. 'Did you get any sleep?'

'Yes,' I say.

'Flynn, what happened? Did you stop taking your lithium?' Her voice shakes.

'No,' I reply truthfully.

She stares at me, her eyes registering first shock, then disbelief. 'What did the psychiatrist say?'

'I've got to go onto a stronger dose.'

'I–I should have seen it.' Jennah is stumbling. 'You – you started being different, you started getting really hyper, and – and really agitated. But I just thought you were in one of your annoying moods . . .' She bites her lip and looks away.

'I'm sorry about yesterday,' I say.

She reaches out and touches my hand. I take her

hand in mine. Something starts at the back of my throat. I bite my tongue. My eyes feel hot.

'Harry and Kate's living room does actually look as if it belongs in the Tate Modern,' Jennah says with a smile. 'You weren't far off the mark with that one.'

A hot tear escapes down my cheek. I swipe at it.

'Perhaps you're in the wrong profession.' Jennah tries to smile again. 'You're even more creative with paint than with music. Who needs paintbrushes when you can just throw paint at the walls? You could start off a whole new trend in interior design.' Her voice has a desperate edge.

I try to laugh, but it comes out as a sob. Jennah gets up and sits on the edge of the bed. She strokes my arm. 'Flynn, it's going to be all right. You got better before, you're going to get better again, OK?'

I rub the corner of the sheet over my face and make foolish gasping noises.

Jennah strokes my leg. 'So what d'you think? Should we enrol you at the Chelsea Arts College?'

I manage a laugh this time. 'What are they going to do? A-about the mess?'

'Harry's already found a decorator,' Jennah tells me. 'And we'll pay for it as a present.'

'I – I kicked Harry . . .'

'Yeah, well, he'll kick you back when you're feeling better,' Jennah says. 'Now budge up, there's room on this bed for two.'

I move over and she pulls herself up against the headboard. She puts her arms around my waist and snuggles up against me. I bury my face in her hair.

The next morning, at breakfast, I ask the nurse for my clothes. She tells me they have been thrown away. I call Rami on his mobile from a pay phone in the corridor and tell him to bring me a pair of shoes. He says he's working. I tell him, fine, I'm discharging myself and walking home barefoot. He tells me to hold on. Forty-five minutes later he arrives with a shoebox and a tracksuit. I put on the new trainers while Rami goes off in search of a doctor. Ages later he returns with one – a fresh-faced medical student, who gives me a final check-over. I have a key worker – a lady named Joy – who I have to meet with every week. Her job is to keep me 'functional', whatever the hell that means. I also have to start group therapy. Sometime around noon, I am finally discharged.

Rami drives me straight over to an appointment with Dr Stefan. He tries to get me to talk about the painting episode. I stare out of the window and don't reply. He reviews my lithium increase. He agrees with it and prescribes me a short course of sleeping pills as well as a daily course of benzodiazepines to take if I start feeling manic again.

After the appointment, I want to go home to Jennah, but Rami insists on taking me out to lunch.

'You've certainly started off the academic year in dramatic style!' he exclaims, tucking into a large plate of carbonara. 'Let's hope the rest of it isn't quite so eventful.'

I look at him. 'Very funny.'

Rami wipes his mouth on his napkin and munches rapidly. He is so used to having lunch on the go that he doesn't know how to eat at a normal pace. 'Sophie and I would really like it if you would come and stay with us for a bit.'

'No thank you.'

'Seriously, Flynn. This is the worst manic episode you've had. The first doctor at the A&E wanted to section you – have papers signed to hold you in hospital for as long as they see fit. It was only because you reacted so well to the tranquillizer that they would even consider discharging you. And it took some persuading.'

'I said, no thanks.'

'Why don't I drive you home to Sussex then?'

'You told Mum and Dad about this?' My voice begins to rise.

'No, I haven't,' Rami says. 'I figured that Dad's blood pressure could do without the news. But the only way I got you out of the hospital so quickly was by telling them that I was a doctor and would take full responsibility for you. You can't just slot back into your life as if nothing happened. It was pretty scary and even dangerous.'

'I'm fine,' I say quietly, trying hard to keep my voice even. 'They've cranked up the lithium so high I can hardly see straight. I feel like a robot, my feelings have completely evaporated and I couldn't even say boo to a goose. I'm no danger to anyone.'

'I'm not thinking you're a danger to anyone.'

'I'm no danger to myself, then.'

Rami stops, spaghetti-laden fork halfway to his mouth. There is a long pause. 'Are you sure about that?'

I glare at him. 'Oh, for Christ's sake.'

'All I'm saying is, I would feel better if you came and stayed for a while.'

'I'm not putting my life on hold just so you can feel better!' I start to shout. A woman sitting at the next table looks round in alarm.

Rami's voice is thick with carefully controlled calm. 'That's not what I meant and you know it. Manic episodes are often followed by periods of deep depression – which, along with the stronger dose of lithium and the potential side-effects of the tranquillizers, means you shouldn't be on your own right now—'

'I'm not on my own! I live with Jennah, remember?'

Rami picks up his fork with a sigh, defeated. 'OK. Just remember that Jennah has her life too. And the offer of a bed in Watford is always there.'

We finish our meal in silence.

I go back to lectures the following morning. Kate and Harry are overly friendly, overly cheerful. I wish I knew what they were thinking. Jennah keeps saying that they understand but I don't see how they can, when even I don't. In the afternoon, I start group therapy and spend the whole hour practising the fingering to Rachmaninov's Second Piano Concerto against the sides of my chair as a succession of listless individuals recount their life story in excruciating detail.

I want to die.

Chapter Five

JENNAH

At first, Rami said they might have to section him. I imagined him tied down to a bed, his body in spasm as they fed electric currents into his brain. I wasn't really thinking straight at the time. I'd travelled in the ambulance with him. They had hooked him up to a heart monitor and kept asking me what recreational drugs he'd taken. The journey to the hospital was awful. It was taking all three paramedics just to restrain him. He kept thrashing about, screaming at them to get off him. I think he was just afraid, but he wouldn't quieten down enough to listen to what they were saying to him. They injected something into the back of his hand. Seconds before we arrived at the hospital, his kicking became more half-hearted. By the time they were unloading him he had stopped moving altogether and they had to lift him into a wheelchair.

While they were examining him in A&E, Harry and Kate arrived. Shortly after that, Rami appeared. He calmed us all down and went to talk to the doctor and took us up to the ward to see Flynn, who by this time was fast asleep. He looked pale and almost childlike against the hospital pillows. Rami told us that Flynn had been injected with a powerful dose of tranquillizer and said he would be out for the night, so Harry, Kate and I went home.

The next day, Rami picked me up before breakfast. When we arrived on the ward, Flynn's bed was empty. A nurse told us he was being seen by the psychiatrist. While we waited for him to return, Rami bought me coffee. I sat on the chair beside the empty unmade bed, sipping my coffee and trying to keep my hands from shaking. Rami had a stab at polite chit-chat but he looked like he hadn't slept. When Flynn finally returned, I didn't recognize him. I just saw a dishevelled guy with blond hair on end, wearing a creased T-shirt and boxers. His face was white, properly white, and he had violet smudges beneath his eyes. My first thought was, *God, I wonder what's wrong with that guy?* My second thought was, *God, that guy is Flynn.* He seemed to be moving incredibly slowly, as if the earth's gravity had dramatically increased.

Rami left, and Flynn and I had a short, painful conversation. I kept saying to myself, *For heaven's sake don't cry.* It was so hard. Flynn sounded like a stroke victim. I knew it was the effect of the tranquillizer but it was somehow horrifying. There were long pauses between each of his words and his speech was slurred. I tried to make a joke about the whole painting episode, but it massively backfired and almost had him sobbing. I left feeling useless and scared and, for the first time since we'd been going out, totally alone.

Now that he is home, he is different. He won't talk about what happened. Looking exceedingly uncomfortable, Harry informed me that Flynn had written him a letter of apology along with a cheque for the damage. Harry said he didn't know what to do. I said, *Just cash the cheque.* There is a silent agreement between us not to tell anyone else at college about what happened. Flynn only missed a couple of days of lectures so no questions have been asked and we are straight back to the normal routine. It's almost as if the psychotic episode never occurred.

Except that Flynn is different. He is subdued. He is sleeping again. A lot. He says it's one of the side-effects of the increased lithium dose. He is on 1200 milligrams now, seeing the psychiatrist twice a week and constantly having blood tests. He doesn't tell me about any of this, of course, but I read the dosage on the packets in the bathroom drawer. I see the purple and yellow bruises in the crooks of his arms, on the backs of his hands.

Rami calls – frequently. Flynn is monosyllabic with him too and uses the excuse of practice to get away from the phone as quickly as possible. He seems so drugged up and slow. I miss his laughter, his impulsiveness, his wacky sense of humour, even his obsessive practising. It makes me wonder who he actually is. If the old Flynn was ill – courtesy of a chemical imbalance in the brain – is this lithiumed Flynn the real McCoy? Or perhaps both characters are just facets of a hidden, deeper soul that I have yet to meet. I just don't know. Sometimes I fear that the drug-free Flynn – searingly manic, then catastrophically depressed – is who he really is. But because in that form he is not acceptable to conventional society, he has to be drugged so that his emotions are tempered and his behaviour controlled. Perhaps we are blindly living in an Orwellian society where individualism is feared and the biggest pressure is the one to conform. Perhaps Flynn is sane and the rest of the world is mad. The thoughts go round and round in my head.

I try talking to Flynn about these things but he isn't interested. Or else he just doesn't want to talk. He seems to be restricting our conversations to uni, essays, lectures, the contents of the fridge. I want to grab him by the shoulders and shake him and shout, *Tell me what was going through your mind when you covered Harry's living room in black paint! Tell me what's going through your mind right now as you sit hunched over your plate, staring at the kitchen wall!* I don't understand, but what really hurts is that Flynn doesn't even seem to *want* me to understand.

I come back from rehearsal and almost fall over Harry's cello case in the hall. Harry is sitting alone in the kitchen, drinking coffee. I suddenly remember why he is here – to practise the Martinu for the chamber music exam. I am so pleased to see him, it worries me. I dump a couple of supermarket bags on the table and give him a quick peck on the cheek.

'Are you staying for dinner?' I ask.

'Depends what you're making.'

'It's Flynn's turn to cook.'

'Perhaps not then.'

I laugh. 'What have you done with him?'

'He's having a shower. I told him he smelled.'

'Thank you.'

'You're welcome. Not looking too good, is he?'

I finish stocking the fridge. 'You've noticed?'

'Kind of hard not to, Jen.'

Flynn comes in, hair wet and tousled, puts on some more coffee and adds some jacket potatoes to the fish in the oven. He turns round and glares at Harry and me, still sitting at the kitchen table.

'Right, so are we going to rehearse this shitty concert piece, or what?'

'That's the spirit!' Harry chuckles.

'And hello to you too,' I say to Flynn with a smile.

Flynn ignores us both, turning on his heel and striding into the living room. Harry and I exchange looks.

'I guess that's our cue,' he says.

'Has he been in this mood since you arrived?'

Harry nods. 'I have a feeling he'd forgotten about the chamber music exam. He'd certainly forgotten about our rehearsal tonight. I think I woke him when I rang the bell.'

I get up reluctantly and turn down the oven. 'I suppose we may as well get started.'

In the living room, Flynn is sitting on the piano stool, slouched forwards over the closed piano lid, his head resting on his arms. There is a long silence while I set up my music stand and assemble my flute and Harry fetches a stool and erects a makeshift stand for himself on the top of the TV. Harry takes his score out of his bag and tries to put the pages in order. Then he attempts to get the pages to stand up against the mug placed strategically atop the TV. It doesn't work and the sheets scatter onto the carpet. I pull a heavy lever-arch file from the shelf.

'Try this.'

'Thanks. I think I'm missing one of the pages now . . .'

'It's here.' I retrieve it from behind the TV.

The score finally in place, Harry lifts his cello out of its case and starts adjusting the spike. Flynn has his eyes closed. I play a tentative A on my flute. Flynn doesn't move.

Harry has his cello set up now. We both look across at Flynn. 'Do you feel like giving us an A?' I ask him, a touch of sarcasm creeping into my voice.

He opens his eyes and straightens up with a long-suffering look, as if we are irritating children pestering him for sweets. He bangs open the piano lid. Plays a very loud A.

Harry and I tune up quickly.

'Shall we play it through once, to start with?' Harry suggests.

Flynn doesn't say anything.

'Sounds good to me,' I reply. I look over at Flynn. He is rummaging through the piles of scores on the piano top, sending a great many of them shooting down the back. 'I don't even have the fucking music,' he says.

'Don't you know it by heart?' Harry asks. Flynn is renowned for learning new pieces in the blink of an eye.

Flynn gives up his hunt and sits back down. 'Fine, I'll just make it up as I go along.'

Harry glances at me and rolls his eyes. I flash him a sympathetic grin. 'All repeats?' I ask.

'Yes,' Harry says.

There is a pause. I raise my flute to my lips and Harry picks up his bow. Flynn glances round at us briefly, inhales the upbeat and we are away.

It is far from brilliant. We are sorely out of practice and this is not the easiest or the most tuneful of pieces, but our unusual instrument combination means that our repertoire is limited. Harry is sawing grimly away at his cello, wincing whenever the piece rises to a particularly unpleasant crescendo. Flynn is playing shockingly badly – like a robot, devoid of any expression. I am stumbling over the quick succession of complicated harmonics as we claw our way painfully to the end.

There is a heavy silence.

'Good God,' Harry says at last. 'Bohuslav Martinu would turn in his grave.'

'I can't believe we're supposed to have this ready by the end of next month,' I groan.

Flynn plays a horribly dissonant chord with his elbows and starts rubbing his eyes.

Another silence. Harry and I are floundering. Normally Flynn takes the lead in rehearsals – mainly because he is, quite simply, the best musician out of us three. Tonight, however, he seems determined not to play ball.

'Okaaay,' Harry says slowly. 'Let's just focus on the first page, shall we?'

We start playing again. Harry breaks off. 'Ouch, ouch, ouch. We have to come together more on bar eleven. Jen, have you got *avante* there?'

'Yes, d'you want me to *avante* it more?'

'Try it.'

We go again. 'Better, but we need a darker colour on bar nineteen,' I say. 'It's too bland.' I look pointedly at Flynn.

Harry shifts uncomfortably. 'OK, a darker colour,' he says, picking up his bow.

'Not you, *you're* dark enough already,' I say.

We pick up again. There is little improvement.

'It still needs a bit more – um . . .' Harry glances nervously at Flynn.

'Are you going to start doing some phrasing or do

you just want to program it into your keyboard and stick it on repeat?' I suddenly snap.

Harry examines the tip of his shoe with great intent.

'I wasn't the one who chose this turgid crap,' Flynn remarks coldly. 'I doubt very much it'll make any difference whether I phrase it or not.'

'It's a bit late now to start arguing over the piece,' I point out.

'From bar nine?' Harry suggests brightly.

'Seeing as I don't have the music, I haven't the faintest idea which bar you're talking about,' Flynn retorts.

'Sorry, sorry,' Harry says hastily. 'From the C sharp?'

'There *is* more than one,' Flynn points out.

'The first one,' Harry says with barely measured calm. 'Or else we could just continue bickering and simply fail the whole module.'

I catch Harry's eye. 'Well said,' I mutter to him.

Flynn has heard me. He wasn't meant to. He turns from the piano to glare at me, face flushed with fury. Then he slams the piano lid down, jumps up and stalks out of the room.

Harry and I stare at each other. There is a long, drawn-out silence and then we hear the bedroom door bang.

Harry hoists his cello across his lap and begins to release the spike. 'God, Jennah, he's being a real little shit.'

I lay my flute on the carpet and pull my knees to my chest. 'What the hell's got into him? I can't believe he's behaving like a two-year-old! He was just looking for a fight!' I take a deep breath and rest my chin on my knees. Suddenly my throat feels tight.

Harry places his cello in its case and looks at me carefully. 'He's obviously feeling crap at the moment, but that doesn't mean he can take it out on you,' he says. 'D'you want me to try and talk some sense into him?'

I shake my head. 'He won't listen to anyone when he's like this. Christ, what are we going to do about the chamber music exam?'

'We'll try again when he's in a better mood,' Harry says. 'Don't worry about that, Jen. If the worst comes to the worst, Flynn will pull a sickie and you and I will dig up an old Mozart duet.' He closes his cello case and gives me a long look. 'Well, if we're not going to rehearse, I should get back to Kate. Are you going to be all right here tonight?'

I nod.

'Are you sure? You can stay over at ours if you want.'

'Thanks, but I'll be OK.' I sigh. 'Oh God, Harry, I just don't know what to do.'

Harry zips up his music bag and looks at me. 'Have you ever thought . . . ?'

'What?' I ask hopefully.

Harry hesitates. 'That maybe there's nothing you *can* do?'

It is not the answer I'm expecting. I stare at him.

'I mean, maybe – maybe this is what it's going to be like when he gets ill,' Harry continues doggedly. 'He'll have an episode – either of mania or depression – his meds will be tweaked, therapy will be stepped up, and everyone will wait for it to pass. Which, of course, it will do.'

'And so – you're saying I should just weather the storm?'

Harry nods slowly. 'I think so, yes. Otherwise you're going to wear yourself down, trying to help him, trying to make things better, when it's basically out of your control.'

I look at Harry. Somewhere, at the back of my mind, I think he might have a point. But I don't want to admit it. Not yet.

Harry hugs me in the doorway, a quick, comforting warmth, and I watch him get into his car and accelerate down the quiet street. As his red brake lights disappear round the corner, silence descends and I feel suddenly lonely. I wonder if Kate knows how lucky she is. I go back into the kitchen, turn off the oven, put the food out to cool and make myself a cup of hot chocolate. I have no appetite for a solitary dinner. I sit at the kitchen table, sipping my drink and staring out into the black pane of night. Some old friends from music camp who knew Harry, Flynn and me as kids expressed surprise when they first heard I was going out with Flynn. They had always thought I would end up with Harry. I don't know why it comes back to me now.

I finish my hot chocolate, wash my cup, cover the fish slowly congealing on the sideboard and put it in the fridge. There is no light under the bedroom door and so I figure Flynn has gone to bed. Although it's barely ten o'clock, I decide to follow suit – I have an early lecture tomorrow and I'm not in the mood to do anything more productive. So I double lock the front door, switch off the lights, brush my teeth and creep into the bedroom. I fumble around in the dark, getting undressed, pulling my nightie over my head. It's only when I'm about to get under the covers that I'm aware that the curtains are still open, the streetlight falling over an empty bed. My slowly adjusting eyes make out a figure sitting against the wall beneath the window. I switch on the bedside lamp.

'What are you doing?'

He is plugged into his iPod and can't hear me. His eyes squint against the light.

'I thought you'd gone to bed,' I say, louder.

He yanks the earphones out. 'I was just waiting for you and Harry to finish talking about me,' he retorts.

I stare at him, stung. 'What exactly did you expect?'

'For my girlfriend and best mate to bitch about me behind my back, obviously.'

The tension that has been growing inside me all evening rises to my throat. 'You really have a nerve, complaining about me, when you're the one who ruined the whole evening by behaving like a prat! What do you expect? For us to start talking about the weather after you go and storm out of the room like a hormonal teenager?'

He throws his iPod furiously against the foot of the bed and starts to shout. 'I had every right to be pissed off, seeing how the two of you were ganging up on me! That's what you always do, isn't it? "Oh God, what are we going to do about Flynn? He's so crazy." "What are we going to do about Flynn? He's all depressed again." '

'What would you rather we do? Ignore you?' I am kneeling up on the pillows, almost shaking with rage. 'God forbid we should be *concerned* about you! God forbid we should *care* about you!'

'I didn't ask for your bloody concern!' Flynn yells. His face is puce, the cords standing out in his neck. I have never seen him so angry. 'A fat lot of good it does me, having you and Harry witter on about how screwed up I am!'

'We never said you were screwed up! We're just worried about you!'

'Well, save your stupid worry, I don't need it!' Flynn yells. 'Stop trying to be Florence fucking Nightingale!'

There is a silence. I feel as if I have been punched in the stomach. The wind is knocked out of me. I am going to start crying. I need to move fast. I stumble from the bed and pull on my jeans and grab a jumper. I pick up my bag in the corridor and shove my feet into a pair of trainers.

'OK, wait, where are you going?' Flynn is beside me in a flash, his hand on my arm. 'Don't be stupid, Jennah, it's late—'

I jerk myself free and keep on going. He grabs my arm again as I reach the front door.

'Get your hands off me!' I yell.

My voice sounds somewhat hysterical. Flynn backs off, looking alarmed. 'Jennah, come on. Listen—'

I crash out of the front door and run down the staircase and out into the street. The night air is sharp, stinging my bare arms. I walk quickly away, towards the bright lights of the main road, blinded by tears.

Harry and Kate are comforting and sympathetic. Of course I can stay the night, of course it will blow over, and of course I did the right thing by walking out. Hunched up in the corner of the sofa, sipping hot coffee, it takes me some time to stop sniffing and shivering. I feel guilty for having intruded on them just as they were about to go to bed but could think of nowhere else to go. Mum is living in Manchester with her partner now – I can't just go running home. I am so, so tired.

Kate suggests I have a hot bath, which I do. Thawing gently in the steamy tub, I look up at the cracked ceiling and wonder if this is the beginning of the end. Two and a half years is not so bad, I suppose. My eyes fill again with painful tears. Why was Flynn so nasty? That's what I can't get my head around. To lose his temper during the rehearsal was one thing, to accuse Harry and me of ganging up against him was another. But to tell me to stop playing Florence Nightingale! That could only have served one purpose – to wound. And he has certainly succeeded.

I get out, dry myself and pull my nightdress back on. In the living room, Harry helps me open up the sofa bed and lends me an alarm clock. I climb under the covers. The phone on the coffee table suddenly springs into life.

Harry sits down on the armrest and picks up. 'Hello?'

I stretch out beneath the duvet. I wonder if I dare skip my morning lecture.

'Calm down, mate, she's here with us,' Harry is saying. He turns to look at me.

I look up at him and frown, shaking my head vigorously.

'She doesn't feel like talking to you right now,' Harry says.

I am watching Harry's face. The sound of rapid speech comes out of the receiver. Harry is struggling to get a word in. 'Yes, yes, I know . . . Yes, she's spending the night . . . No, don't come round now. We're all going to bed. Get some sleep and call back in the morning.'

More rapid speech.

'Yes, all right . . . But she doesn't want to talk to you just now . . . I'll tell her you called, OK?'

Harry looks at me again. Widens his eyes dramatically. 'No, I really don't think that's a good idea . . . No. Listen, mate, I'll get her to call you tomorrow.'

When Harry finally hangs up, he turns to look at me. 'He sounded upset.'

A sliver of fear runs through me. 'How upset?'

A pause. 'You look knackered, Jen,' Harry says suddenly. 'Get some sleep, OK? Things will seem better in the morning.'

He gets up to go and I pull the duvet around me. 'Harry?'

'Mm?' He stops in the doorway.

'Thank you.'

Chapter Six

FLYNN

'At bar one eighteen,' Professor Kaiser says, 'are you playing it *accelerando* with intention?'

I am not doing anything with intention. I am just trying to get through this lesson without popping a blood vessel.

'Keep it *a battuta* until the E flat,' the professor continues. 'Let the notes maintain their weight until the quaver passage after the F sharp.'

I don't know what the fuck he is talking about. The only weight I am aware of is inside my head. I didn't sleep last night. I bought a bottle of vodka and a packet of cigarettes and watched in a blurry, drunken haze as a watery dawn rose over the rooftops. Now I am playing in a winter jacket in Kaiser's under-heated study at the end of a wet, rainy day; the professor pacing the room like a caged animal as I attack Rachmaninov's Second Piano Concerto with barely concealed hatred.

'*Da pum pum pum . . .*' Kaiser repeats the fingering of the runaway semi-quavers on the top of the piano. 'Keep – the – tempo,' he chants in time to the imaginary notes.

I throw myself back into the semi-quavers to drown out the sound of Kaiser's voice.

But Kaiser just starts to shout. 'Flynn! *A battuta!* Quavers, not semi-quavers!'

I close my eyes and try and shut him out. My fingers don't want to stay in time. They want to race ahead in fury, plunging into the dense fog of black notes, pulling the music out by its roots, hurling it up out of the piano and into the air. I dive into the fat staccato chords like a madman with a hammer, pounding the notes out of the grand piano until the floor shakes. I collapse at the end of the first movement, my forehead hitting the piano ledge with a thud.

'Very theatrical, Flynn,' Kaiser says dryly as the final chord hangs in the air. 'But I'm not sure that is exactly what Rachmaninov meant when he wrote *decrescendo.* We need some element of control or the piece loses its centre. The staccato chords need more space – *pum, pum, pum.* They are sounding more like quarter notes than two whole notes tied. You need to massage them and then use pedal, get them to ooze . . .'

I stare at a spot on the wall just above a portrait of Handel and try and remove the thought of oozing chords from my mind.

'Show me,' Kaiser is saying. 'Milk the chords—'

'From where?' I snap irritably. My head is killing me.

'The cadences, of course.' Professor Kaiser looks at me in surprise.

'OK, OK. From the G sharp?'

'The B flat.'

I take a deep breath and dive back in. The sound crashes about the room like a stormy sea. I can't for the life of me remember why I ever agreed to learn this piece. I am sure that music was never meant to sound this harsh, this painful.

'Whoa, whoa!' Professor Kaiser shouts.

I pretend not to hear him.

'Clarity! Clarity!' he shouts again.

I lose my fingering and jolt to a dissonant halt. 'What?' I bark furiously.

'Even in eruptions of *fortissimo,* you need to take more time to ensure *clarity,*' Kaiser says.

'What are you talking about?' I snap. 'I've got pedal markings till the end of this whole section!'

'What I mean is—'

'You want it without the pedal now?' I demand furiously. 'Or you want it with pedal but without *sostenuto* and clear within the resonance?' I can hear my heart.

The professor stops his pacing and turns, looking at me thoughtfully. 'I think you are more excited than even the music today, no?' He considers me for a moment.

I breathe. I realize I have been shouting and I can feel the heat pounding in my cheeks. I gnaw at my thumbnail.

'Let's stop for today. We can keep the clarity-within-resonance problem for next time,' Professor Kaiser suggests gently. 'You look tired.'

I busy myself, gathering my music together.

'I can tell things are difficult at the moment . . .'

My teeth are clenched together so hard, my jaw aches. Does the whole world know? I mumble something not even I can hear.

As I pull the strap of my bag across my chest and move towards the door, Professor Kaiser puts a restraining hand on my arm. 'Flynn—'

'I'm OK!' I jump away violently. 'I'm OK. Really. Thanks for the lesson. I'll see you tomorrow, as usual.' And I turn and hurry from the room, away from the menacing threat of his concern.

I buy a packet of cigarettes and chain-smoke them on a damp bench in the park, a mini-gale buffeting around me. I've smoked so much in the last twenty-four hours that the taste makes me feel sick, but I feel like doing something self-destructive. It's funny how you can think you've reached rock bottom, then sink a whole lot further. I know I only have myself to blame but that is little consolation. Yesterday evening Harry and Jennah made me so angry, and I hardly know why. Something to do with their friendship, which has always been very close. Something to do with the realization that Jennah has more in common with Harry than with me. Something to do with the fact that I am depressed, and they are not. Something to do with them being the long-suffering friends and I the pain-in-the-neck. Something to do with wishing I was anyone but me.

I don't know where the stupid Florence Nightingale remark came from. I regretted it as soon as the words were out. I just grabbed at the first nasty taunt I could think of. I wanted to hurt Jennah; to make her see, just for a second, what it felt like to really hurt. How evil that sounds. To want to make someone you love suffer the way you suffer. I am cruel and selfish and envious. I hate myself more than they could ever hate me.

I am so, so sick of it. This is the overriding feeling. They say depression is an incredible sadness, an unbearable mental pain. No, it doesn't have to be so dramatic. Sometimes it is nothing more than feeling tired. Tired of life. In therapy they tell you to remember that the bad spells pass. That things do get better, that medication does work, that things don't stay the same. I can't see how this is supposed to help. Ultimately everything ends with death. What they should say is: things might get better for a while, but eventually you will go back to being nothing, and all the pain and suffering will have been in vain. I wonder what Dr Stefan would have to say to that. They say that depression makes you see everything in a negative light. I disagree. It makes you see things for what they are. It makes you take off the fucking rose-tinted glasses and look around and see the world as it really is – cruel, harsh and unfair. It makes you see people in their true colours – stupid, shallow and self-absorbed. All that ridiculous optimism, all that *carpe diem* and life's-what-you-make-of-it. Words, just empty words in an attempt to give meaning to an existence that is both doomed and futile.

I need to walk. When I start thinking like this, I scare even myself. Because I know I'm right, and because I know there is only one way out. There are people you're supposed to call when you're feeling like this. The Samaritans, my psychiatrist . . . Why? So they can talk you out of it? Talk you out of 'harming' yourself? It's all rubbish. I'm harmed already. I only want to be kind to myself, to put myself out of my misery.

I walk quickly, even though I have nowhere to go. My warm breath mingles with the cigarette smoke, creating small white clouds against the cold air. It has been raining, and everything is wet and sharp and new. Cars swish by, their lights picking out the puddles on the pavement. A weary chill settles in between my shoulder blades. The hand holding the cigarette is soon numb with cold. Autumn has turned into winter.

My mobile erupts into a series of clamorous vibrations. I pull it hurriedly out of my jacket pocket in the vain hope that it will be Jennah's name on the caller ID. It's Rami. I flick the phone open without thinking. 'What?'

'Hello. Nice to hear from you too.'

'I'm busy.'

'Doing what?'

'Practising.'

'You're outside – I can hear the wind.'

'I'm on my way home to practise.'

'Well, you can talk to me till you get there, can't you?'

'I don't need you calling me every fucking day to check up on me!'

A weary pause. 'That's a bit of an exaggeration. What's going on, Flynn?'

'Nothing!'

'Is the dose too high?'

'How the hell should I know?'

'There's always a massive come-down after a manic episode, you know that,' Rami reminds me, his voice heavy with infuriating moderation. 'And your body's having to adjust to the increased dose in medication, so you're getting a double whammy of depression right now. It'll pass, Flynn.'

'Who the hell said I was depressed?'

There is silence at the other end of the line and I picture Rami biting his lip, trying to resist saying something funny but sarky that will cause me to hang up on him.

After Rami finishes quizzing me about my mood, side-effects, psych appointments and all the fucking rest, I leave the park and find myself heading towards Harry's. My pride tells me I should go home and wait it out, but a strange mix of self-destruction and despair keeps me going. I have sunk so low now, it almost entertains me to try to sink further. I pass a homeless guy in a damp sleeping bag and realize with a jolt that there is precious little standing between him and me. A girlfriend who doesn't return, a couple of months' missed rent, clothes that haven't been changed for a few weeks.

An emptied-out bank account, the last of the student loan spent on fags and booze, parents who don't know what to do any more . . .

I press the buzzer to Harry's flat and rest my forehead against the wet intercom. Harry's voice crackles out. 'Yep?'

'Let me in. It's Flynn.'

Brief hesitation. 'Uh – just hold on a sec.'

'For fuck sake!' I kick the door. 'Just let me in, will you?'

'OK, OK.' The buzzer sounds and I shove open the door and go up the stairs.

Harry is standing in the doorway. 'She's not here, you know.'

I glare at him. 'I don't believe you.'

He sighs wearily and holds open the door. 'You can come and search the flat if you want to. I think she's still at uni. Doesn't she have lectures till five on a Thursday?'

I stop and think. 'Oh yeah. Shit.'

'You may as well come in,' Harry says. 'Coffee?'

'OK.' We go into the kitchen. Harry puts the kettle on.

I run my hands through my hair and look around to see if any of Jennah's things are still here. 'So, is she planning on sleeping here again tonight?'

'I've no idea,' Harry says.

'What, she didn't tell you anything? She didn't tell you if she was coming back here or not?'

Harry sits down at the table. 'I didn't see her this morning, Flynn. I had a lesson at ten and by the time I got home, she'd left.' He looks at me. 'Sit down, man, you look rough. Do you want something to eat?'

'No. She must have given you some idea—'

'Look, I really don't know,' Harry says, getting up to pour the coffee. 'Have you tried her mobile?'

'Obviously! It's been off all day!'

'Well then, she's still in lectures,' Harry says. 'Or . . .' He hesitates.

'What?' I challenge him.

'Or she doesn't want to speak to you.' He glances at me nervously. 'Probably she's still in lectures.'

'Why wouldn't she want to speak to me?' I demand.

'I dunno, Flynn. She seemed pretty upset last night.'

'We had a *fight*,' I say. 'That's what couples *do*. Shit happens! She needs to learn to deal with it.'

'Right.' Harry sets down a mug of coffee in front of me, infuriatingly calm. 'One bit of advice though – don't say that to her.'

I take an angry gulp of coffee, scalding my tongue. 'Did she sleep here last night?'

'You know she did—'

'What did she *say*?'

'Nothing. Just that you'd had a row.'

'Why did she have to spend the night here? Why couldn't she spend the night at home? Why did she have to come running to you and Kate, for Christ's sake? How are we supposed to resolve our differences if she won't even talk about them?'

'Maybe she just wanted a little space.' Harry holds up his hands. 'Hey. I'm not acting as go-between here. Jen's a mate – if you'd needed a bed for the night I'd have done the same for you. My guess is she's on her way home now. So go and sort it out. But for God's sake, calm down and stop shouting.'

I finish my coffee in silence. Harry is looking at me with an expression similar to Professor Kaiser's. It irritates the hell out of me.

I stop off at the supermarket on the way home. I figure one way of saying sorry might be by cooking dinner. I stagger down the narrow hallway under the weight of the bags and find Jennah curled up on the sofa.

'Hello.'

'Hi.' She glances at me fleetingly. She is watching TV, an unreadable expression on her face.

I dump the bags in the kitchen, pull out the bunch of roses I picked up from the florist at the end of the road, and go back into the living room.

'These are to say sorry.'

She gives me a long look. Fights a smile. 'Oh, Flynn . . .'

'I was a bastard.'

'You really were,' she agrees, taking the flowers from me and laying them down on the coffee table. 'And that's not like you.' She kneels up and puts her arms round me. 'What's going *on* with you?'

I give an embarrassed shrug. 'Nothing. I was just cranky.'

'Cranky, huh?' She begins to laugh. 'That's the word for it. God, you were like a bear with a sore head! I don't know how we're ever going to persuade Harry to practise the trio with us again.'

'We will.' I squint down at her. 'Am I allowed a kiss?'

'I'm considering it . . .'

'If I cook dinner?'

She gives in with a smile.

The thought of dinner only comes back to me sometime later as we lie on the sofa, our clothes strewn about the living-room floor.

'Sex makes me hungry,' Jennah says.

I bite her nose. 'Your wish is my command.'

'Are you going to cook naked?'

'No way! Valuable things might get burned!'

At Jennah's insistence, we eat dinner by candlelight. She reaches across the table and holds my hand throughout the meal. We talk about unimportant stuff – the Purcell Room concert, plans for Christmas, Kate's new haircut . . . As she chats away, the candlelight is reflected in her pupils, making them shine like cats' eyes. When she smiles, her nose crinkles and dimples appear in her cheeks. I look at her, stare at her, and I think: I wish I could pick you up and put you in my pocket. I wish I could carry you with me all the time, safe and warm. I wish there was a way I could be with you all the time, every hour of every day. Each time you smile, it's like the first time all over again, and my heart flutters in my chest. I want to reach out and hold you – it's like a physical ache. I want to stroke your face and kiss your eyelashes and feel your skin and smell your hair. I love you. I love you so much. And it hurts. I don't know why.

Jennah breaks off from a long story involving a fellow student and a sleazy university lecturer and props her chin up on her hand. 'What?'

I meet her eyes, startled. 'Nothing.'

'You're giving me that look . . .' She narrows her eyes at me in mock-suspicion.

I shake my head in embarrassment. 'I'm just listening to you—'

'No you're not.' She catches me out instantly. 'What are you thinking?'

I shoot her a look. 'Stuff.'

She smiles. 'Ah, stuff.' She nods knowingly, musingly. 'That's very interesting, very interesting indeed. I've always wanted to know more about *stuff*.'

'Ha ha.'

Her smile flickers. 'Why won't you tell me?'

I look away, scraping the last bits of onion from my plate. 'It's not that. It's just not important. I'm not thinking about anything really—'

'Flynn . . .' She cuts me off.

I look at her. 'You really want to know?'

She nods.

I inhale sharply. 'OK. What I'm thinking is that all this – all this will one day be just a memory—'

'A nice memory.' Jennah smiles.

'No, a painful memory. A painful memory that I'm going to spend a lifetime trying to forget and – and failing.'

Her smile dies. 'Flynn . . .'

'No, listen. You wanted to know. All this is transient, everything is transient. Nothing lasts. Nothing is for ever. I can't hold onto you. I can only love you. And what's the point of loving you if it means someday I have to lose you? How am I supposed to enjoy my life while the whole time I'm waiting for that to happen?' My voice is rising.

Jennah stares at me long and hard, her smile gone. 'Why?' she says softly. 'Why do you have to *do* this?'

'Do what? *What* am I doing?'

'Spoiling it. Thinking these miserable thoughts. Seeing only the negative—'

'Because it's the truth!' I exclaim loudly.

Jennah gets up. 'Flynn, if you're going to start shouting—'

'I'm not – I'm not!' I sidestep her, blocking her exit, putting my hand on her arm. 'You're the one who asked me. I'm just trying to *explain*.'

She looks at me almost pityingly. 'What do you want, Flynn? For me to say, *Yes, you're right, there's no point to anything, we may as well all shoot ourselves now*?'

'Yes . . . No! I just want to make you see . . .'

‘See what? That it’s all useless?’

I stop, dropping my arms down by my sides. ‘Yes.’

There is a long silence. I am still standing in the doorway, the heat in my cheeks, breathing too fast. ‘You see, you know it too,’ I say.

Jennah says nothing and starts clearing the plates.

‘What? You think I’m crazy, don’t you?’

She stops, looking up at me from beneath a curtain of hair. ‘I think you’re depressed, Flynn.’

I swallow. ‘Maybe. But that doesn’t mean I’m not *right.*’

She drops the plates into the sink and turns round. ‘It’s not about right or wrong, it’s about perspective.’

‘OK. But mixed up in all the different perspectives is some kind of universal truth.’

Jennah closes her eyes and lets out an exaggerated groan. ‘Please, Flynn, it’s nearly midnight, it’s too late to be talking about universal truths—’

‘OK – OK.’ I hold up my hands, leaning against the door, defeated.

Jennah dries her hands on the tea-towel, comes over to me and puts her arms round my neck. ‘Good things don’t always have to end. People do find ways of staying together all their lives. It *has been done before.*’ She gives me a teasing smile, her eyes begging me to respond.

‘Yeah, I know, I know,’ I reply, pulling her close. ‘I’m being daft. All I’m really trying to say is I don’t want to lose you.’

We do the dishes together, flicking foam at each

other, back to the earlier chit-chat and playful teasing. Later we brush our teeth and get undressed and argue over the alarm clock setting and collapse into bed. Nothing really matters – Jennah is smiling again, everything is fine. There is no need to tell her about the wall of darkness inside my mind.

Chapter Seven

JENNAH

Rami rings one evening while Flynn is out at a piano lesson. The baby is yelling lustily in the background. Raising his voice over the sound of his daughter's wails, Rami asks me what our plans are for Christmas.

'Haven't really had a chance to discuss it,' I confess. 'Mum's staying in Manchester for Christmas with her partner Alan and his two sons, so I guess I'll be playing happy step-families with all of them. Flynn, I imagine, will be going to Sussex with you and Sophie.'

'Well, I spoke to my parents this morning,' Rami says, 'and they would really love it if you would come and spend Christmas with us.'

'Really?' I am touched, even though my heart lurches slightly at the thought of spending my first Christmas away from Mum. 'Then I could go home on Boxing Day instead and miss the mayhem. Are you sure that wouldn't be an imposition?'

'Absolutely not. They'd love to have you. We all would.'

* * *

When Flynn comes in, looking drained as usual from his lesson with Kaiser, I relay the conversation to him. He stares at me in disbelief. 'You're kidding me.'

I look at him, stung by his reaction. 'No, I'm not. But if the idea fills you with horror, we can easily change it.'

He pulls himself together sharply. 'No, no, of course not. That's great.'

'You're such a bad liar,' I retort. 'It's fine, I'll just tell Rami my mother wants me home for Christmas.'

'No, Jennah, come on. I was surprised, that's all, surprised that Rami had organized it without . . . Anyway, let's do it. It'll be fun.' He says the word 'fun' as if it were synonymous with 'agony'. 'I just – I'm just not a big fan of Christmas, that's all.'

I relent, pouting. 'Humbug. Do you even know what you're going to get me yet?'

He flushes suddenly. 'Yep.'

'Really?' I crow. 'What? Oh, give me one tiny clue. Please, please! Have you bought it already?'

He averts his eyes. 'Maybe.'

'Tell me!'

'Yeah, right. If I tell you, it will be like that scene in *Friends* where Rachel and Phoebe run around turning the flat upside down, trying to find Monica's hidden presents.'

'So you *have* bought it!'

'I didn't say that.'

I put my arms round his neck. 'But you insinuated it!'

He gives me a lopsided smile. 'Enough silliness,' he says firmly. 'I might change my mind and take it back. Now what we should really be discussing is what *you're* going to get *me*.'

There is so much going on in the run-up to the end of term that it feels as if Flynn and I hardly see each other. What with rehearsals for the Purcell Room concert, rehearsals for the Christmas recital, coursework deadlines, end-of-term drinks and the usual diet of lectures and classes, there is barely time to come up for breath. We laugh when we meet in corridors at the Royal College and greet each other with 'Hello, stranger' and 'Do I know you?', only occasionally having time to stop for lunch with Harry and Kate. Flynn seems OK, back to his normal self; the new dose appears to be working. I feel like I'm constantly running, continually late for something, invariably meant to be somewhere else five minutes ago. I sing *Laudate Dominum* in the Purcell Room without any major hitches. I manage to survive a horribly difficult orchestra piece with the Royal College Symphonia. I try and persuade my two Saturday morning pupils that the flute can actually sound quite nice if you take the trouble to practise between lessons. I turn in half a dozen coursework assignments and finally find myself washed up on the holiday shore, essay-weary and socially depleted.

On Christmas Eve, Rami and Sophie swing by to pick us up in their Ford Focus, baby Aurora asleep in the back. As Flynn loads our rucksacks into the boot, I squeeze up against the car seat and kiss Aurora's sweet-smelling, downy cheek. Flynn climbs into the back beside me and we are off, heading down through the city, leaving an already darkening central London behind us.

'So how are the two musicians?' Rami asks jovially from behind the wheel.

'Very relieved to be leaving our instruments behind,' I reply.

'I bet it's been a mad term,' Sophie says. 'Remember, Rami, how at medical school they always piled on the work just before Christmas?'

'I do,' Rami says. 'God, imagine having to write an essay now. I wouldn't know where to start.'

'I can't believe how big Aurora is!' I exclaim.

'That's because she never stops eating. I swear she's going to become the first obese one-year-old Watford has ever seen and they'll make a programme about her on the Discovery Channel,' Sophie says.

'She's not fat!' I protest. 'Just chubby. Like all babies should be. And all those blonde curls! She's just *so gorgeous.*'

'Yes, she *is* at her best when she's asleep,' Rami observes drily.

I laugh.

'How are you, Flynn?' Sophie enquires.

'OK.'

'I'm sorry I couldn't make it to your last recital,'

Sophie says. 'But Rami told me you kicked up a standing ovation.'

'Yeah, it was OK.'

'More than OK from what I heard.'

We drift into comfortable silence. I like Sophie a lot. She is warm and motherly and has this knack of making you feel important. She feels like an older sister. I look across at Flynn. He is resting his elbow on the ledge below the window, chewing his nails, staring out. The passing cars create a pattern of moving lights across his face.

Aurora sleeps like an angel for the whole journey and only wakes when the engine is switched off and the car doors open. Flynn's parents, Matias and Maria, come out to the car to greet us in their woolly jumpers and slippers, hugging themselves against the freezing night air. Maria gives me a hug and Matias his usual firm handshake, and then everyone is fighting over who gets to carry the bags, and Rami is saying, 'For heaven's sake, Mum, put it down,' and to my delight I am given the baby. Mayhem continues as we all traipse into the narrow hallway of the cottage, and there are overnight bags underfoot and Aurora's travel cot blocking the stairs. Eventually we all get our belongings up to our respective bedrooms – Flynn and I are sharing a fold-out bed in Matias's study – and we regroup in the living room, where Sophie is breast-feeding and Matias is pouring coffee.

Although it is the first time I have been to their

home, I know Matias and Maria quite well from all the concerts and competitions we have attended together. Matias is an older version of Rami but stockier and with a shock of white hair. Maria is an elegant woman with long grey hair tied up in a bun and arresting blue eyes. They both speak English with an accent from their native Finland and sometimes switch into Finnish for no apparent reason, the sound of which never ceases to impress me. I tried to get Flynn to teach me some Finnish when we first started going out, but it didn't take me long to realize why it's considered one of the world's most difficult languages.

I follow Maria into the kitchen and help her set the table for dinner. Something is crackling on the stove and the small room is filled with a warm fug and the smell of fried meat. As I take the glasses down from the cupboard, Maria looks at me and smiles. 'Your hair has grown since I last saw you. It suits you.'

'Thanks.' I can feel myself blush.

'You must be tired,' Maria says.

'A bit. The end of term is always frantic.'

Maria wipes her hands on a tea towel and stirs something on the stove. 'This term must have been particularly difficult . . . with Flynn not being well.'

I look at her. 'You know about that?'

'I guessed. He sounded very agitated on the phone. I finally got Rami to confess that he'd spent a couple of nights in hospital.' She looks suddenly drawn. 'I tried and tried to persuade Flynn to come home for a break, but he wouldn't. He doesn't listen to me any more, Jennah. Or to his father. He doesn't even listen to Rami. But he listens to you.'

There is a pause. Setting out the plates, I search for something to say. It is difficult to express sympathy without being disloyal to Flynn. Maria hasn't moved from her position by the stove. She looks tired, defeated somehow.

'We are so grateful to you,' she adds suddenly, so quietly I'm not sure if I've heard correctly. 'But your mother must be very worried . . .'

I say nothing and finish setting the table. No, my mother isn't worried about me. My mother suffered an acrimonious divorce when I was a baby and is naturally suspicious of men, especially men who go out with her only child. My mother could not cope with the knowledge that her daughter's boyfriend was suffering from a serious mental illness.

We eat something called *vorschmack* round the kitchen table. Aurora is perched on her mother's knee, slobbering over a piece of sausage. Matias asks me about uni, about my concert, about my teaching jobs. I notice for the first time that he has the same lopsided smile as Flynn. Maria coos over Aurora, between jumping up every few minutes to offer people more food, and talks to Sophie about stretch marks and sore nipples. Rami asks his dad for some advice on tax returns and I turn to Flynn, who for most of the meal has been completely mute.

'This is so nice,' I say to him with a smile.

He smiles back, a vacant look in his eyes.

After dinner Rami passes Aurora round the table for a goodnight kiss, then takes her upstairs to bed. Sophie and I join Maria and Matias in the living room for coffee, while Flynn stays behind in the kitchen to attack the washing up, almost aggressive in his refusal of help. When Rami comes back down and joins us, the conversation turns to baby-rearing, and I pick up my coffee and return to the kitchen. I put my hand on Flynn's back and look at his reflection in the darkened pane of the kitchen window. His head is down and I can't see his expression.

'I don't need any help,' Flynn says.

'I haven't come to help. I've come to talk to you,' I say.

Silence. More scrubbing.

'Is everything OK?' I ask.

'Of course. You?'

'Yes, your parents are so sweet. Your mum's gone to such trouble with all the Christmas decorations and everything, hasn't she?'

He nods.

'Are you tired?' I ask.

'Bit.'

'Me too. Do you want to go to bed after this?'

'Yeah.'

I stop talking. Gaze unseeingly at Flynn's reflection in the black window. Even though we are standing side by side, there is an abyss between us.

* * *

Christmas morning I wake early in the squeaky, unfamiliar bed as a cold dawn filters in between the curtains. Flynn's side of the bed is empty and his clothes are gone from the chair. I yawn and stretch and get up slowly, padding about on the threadbare carpet, the floorboards creaking beneath my feet. I draw the curtains and make the bed and then go to the bathroom to wake myself with a hot shower.

In the kitchen downstairs only Sophie is up, along with Aurora, much to my delight. 'Merry Christmas, Sophie! Merry Christmas, baby boo!' I kiss the top of her warm head. Aurora is sitting on the side of the kitchen table, a tea towel tied around her neck. Sophie is spooning something white and runny into her mouth.

'She's like clockwork, this one,' Sophie explains with a tired smile. 'She doesn't do weekends or holidays.' Aurora grins a toothless grin and flaps her arms in agreement.

'Coffee?' I ask.

'That would be lovely.'

I go over to put on the kettle. 'Have you seen Flynn this morning?'

'Yes, he went out about half an hour ago. For a walk, I think he said.'

'Oh.' We lapse into silence. Aurora gurgles happily as Sophie continues to feed her and I sit and tickle her foot.

'How are things, Jen?' Sophie asks suddenly.

'Fine,' I reply instantly. 'Why?'

'You seem' – a pause – 'a little subdued.'

'It's been a crazy term,' I reply.

'I bet. You do know that if ever you or Flynn need a break from the city, or from each other, our guest room is ready and waiting.'

I smile, stroking Aurora's podgy arm. 'That's kind. Thanks.'

'It's not always easy, living with someone,' Sophie continues. 'I remember when Rami and I first moved in together, I used to get terrible cabin fever every few weeks and have to run home to my mum.'

I laugh. 'Yeah, it does take a bit of getting used to. Especially when you live in a tiny flat like ours.'

'It's such a cosy flat, though,' Sophie says. 'You've both made it really nice.'

'Yeah.' I think back to last summer, when Flynn and I moved in. How different things were then. We had both been full of energy and excitement, combing the second-hand shops for furniture and knick-knacks. It seems like a lifetime ago.

I get up to make the coffee. Aurora babbles happily and blows white spit bubbles. Sophie gets up and wipes her daughter down, then puts her on the floor with some toys and starts a game of peek-a-boo. I hand Sophie her coffee and join them on the carpet.

'Rami seems like a really hands-on dad,' I say.

Sophie smiles. 'Oh, he is. I think he was a bit paranoid when she was a newborn – kept checking her for every possible illness in the book! But now that she's bigger, he's much more relaxed.'

I take the plastic keys that Aurora is holding out to me. 'Thank you, baba!'

'And Flynn is a lovely uncle,' Sophie adds.

'Yeah,' I say, concentrating on Aurora.

A pause. 'He doesn't seem too well at the moment, does he?'

'No . . .'

Aurora shakes the plastic keys and gurgles happily.

'That can't be easy,' Sophie says.

I hold out a teddy to Aurora and tickle her with it under her chin. 'I thought the lithium was supposed to keep him well.' I don't look at Sophie. 'He's been fine ever since he started the medication two and a half years ago. But now . . .' I tail off as Aurora attempts to grasp the bear between her podgy hands.

'Are you worried about him?' Sophie asks.

'Yes – no – I don't know,' I flounder. 'He won't talk, he won't tell me. I just don't understand how someone can be so happy one week and then so miserable the next. I know it's all about the chemicals in his brain but surely we're more than just fluctuating chemicals . . .'

'Of course we are,' Sophie says. 'There is still so much we don't understand about the brain.'

'Sometimes I think it's just him,' I say. 'I know this sounds really mean, but sometimes I think that he could control it if he wanted to, because we all have good days and bad days, don't we?'

'Yes, but we don't all start throwing paint around when we're having a good day and stay in bed when we're having a bad day. We might feel like doing those things' – Sophie smiles – 'but we don't. That, I suppose, is the difference.'

Gradually the rest of the house comes to life. I play with Aurora while Sophie goes off to get dressed. Rami soon joins us and gives Aurora a second breakfast. I help Maria peel the potatoes and baste the turkey. Rami and Matias try and fix something on the living-room computer. Flynn comes in, his cheeks pink from the cold. Breakfast is drawn out over most of the morning while the oven hums and slowly fills the kitchen with the warm smell of roasting. We all crowd round while Aurora opens the first of her presents. She chews happily on the wrapping paper while Rami and Sophie endeavour to assemble some kind of complicated toy.

We play Scrabble in front of the TV; Sophie tries to distract Aurora from eating the Scrabble tiles with an offering of further presents. Flynn sits slightly apart from us all, leaning against the leg of a chair, knees drawn up. He smiles and stretches out his leg to tickle Aurora with his big toe. Finally, at three, we sit down to lunch and pull crackers and drink plum wine. It is a lovely, mellow day.

After lunch we assemble in the living room and exchange presents. I hand Flynn his present from me – a silver envelope containing tickets to *The Contenders* at the National. It is a play Flynn mentioned wanting to see last month. I get some books, a cashmere jumper and, from Flynn, a pair of beautiful silver pendant earrings.

I kneel up to give him a kiss. 'Thank you. They're beautiful!'

He smiles with a distant look in his eyes.

Maria thanks us for the gloves and Matias seems pleased with the aftershave. Rami wraps the bright multicoloured scarf around his neck and tells us it will cheer him up on cold, grey mornings. To my great relief, Sophie hasn't read *I Don't Know How She Does It* and laughs at the title. Aurora chews contentedly on the ear of her talking teddy.

After all the presents are unwrapped and cooed over, Flynn goes into the kitchen to make coffee. Maria turns up the sound on the TV and Rami and I start clearing up the mess of wrapping paper and coloured ribbons.

'Hey, whose is this?' Rami suddenly asks, retrieving an envelope from a swirl of reindeer paper and holding it aloft. I recognize my silver envelope containing the theatre tickets. My present to Flynn. The envelope is still sealed, discarded, tossed in with the rest of the rubbish.

'It's mine,' I say quickly. Rami chucks it over and I stuff it into my pocket.

Later in the evening, Sophie and Rami are trying to organize a game of Pictionary, Matias is dosing off in his armchair, and Flynn has disappeared on another walk.

Maria suddenly turns to me and says, '*Kulta,* you should go and phone your mother.'

I glance at my watch, trying to work out what stage of the proceedings Alan and his kids will have reached, and say, 'OK, perhaps I'll give her a call now.'

'You can use the phone in our bedroom,' Maria says. 'It'll be quieter there.'

'No, it's OK, I've got my mobile,' I protest.

'Mobiles are expensive! Use our landline,' she insists.

I smile my thanks and go upstairs. In the quiet, cool bedroom, I sit on the edge of the double bed and lift the receiver.

'Darling!' Mum sounds overjoyed. I can hear the television, along with a great deal of talking and laughing in the background. 'I've been waiting to call all day but didn't want to interrupt anything. Oh, we've missed you so much. It hasn't been the same without you. My little girl, all grown up. I've been thinking about you non stop. Next year you and Flynn are coming here, promise, OK? Alan cooked us an amazing lunch – roast turkey, stuffing and all – can you believe it? The boys actually offered to do the washing-up, and now they're embroiled in an inter-galactic war. Are you having a really good time?'

'Oh yeah, you know, it's been great . . .' I tail off. Suddenly I'm finding it difficult to speak.

'Did you have a nice lunch?' Mum presses me. 'Who cooked?'

'Flynn's mum. Yeah, it was lovely.' I stare hard at the

patterned pale blue wallpaper. Suddenly I'm overcome by a dreadful feeling of homesickness. Why did I choose to spend Christmas here? Flynn wouldn't have noticed either way.

'Did you get anything nice?' Mum asks.

'Yes.' I dig my nails into the palm of my hand. *What is the matter with you?* 'I'll – I'll show you when I come up.'

'I'm longing to see you tomorrow – we've got your presents here, under the tree,' Mum says. 'You're getting in at four-oh-five, aren't you?'

'Yes,' I say weakly. 'Will you come and fetch me?'

'Of course I will! I'll be waiting for you outside in the car. Won't Flynn change his mind and come too?'

'No, he's got to go back to London and practise,' I say.

'Well, the boys are going home tomorrow so it will just be the three of us,' Mum says. 'Nice and peaceful. Can't wait, darling.'

'OK. See you tomorrow, then . . .' My voice falters. 'Bye.'

'Bye!'

I replace the receiver and stare at the framed photo on the nightstand. The smiling little blond boy in the paddling pool looks a lot like Flynn. It is an effort to hold back the tears.

Another long meal stretches well into the evening. I feel cut off, trapped inside my own air bubble. Everyone is in high spirits except for Flynn, who scarcely even looks my way. I finally manage to extract myself from the cheery fug of the kitchen, leaving Flynn at the sink again. I brush my teeth and strip down to my T-shirt and pants and crawl into the squeaky camp-bed, aching with relief. Dinner was a painful effort, having to act all cheery and chatty despite the constant ache at the back of my throat. I leave the bedside light on for Flynn and pull the duvet over my head, wishing there was a way to shut out the whole world.

Sometime later, teetering on the edge of consciousness, I am aware of the bedroom door opening and closing, the sound of shoes and jeans being kicked off, then finally the squeak of springs and the weight on the mattress beside me. I open my eyes in the sudden darkness, waiting to see if Flynn will kiss me goodnight. He doesn't. He doesn't even touch me. I close my eyes again. The silver envelope is still in the pocket of my denim skirt. Tomorrow I will throw it away.

I wake with the dawn chorus. Flynn's arm is slung across me, a heavy weight over my chest. I get dressed quietly and pad to the bathroom. The house sleeps. Even Aurora isn't yet clamouring to be entertained. I take the key from the kitchen drawer and let myself out of the house. The village lane is lit by a cold, bluish dawn. Despite my long black winter coat, the chill bites at my skin. It has rained in the night – there are wet leaves and slippery mud underfoot. I walk rapidly through the village. I don't know where I'm going, I just know that I need to walk, move, feel alive. Flynn has turned into an empty shell. He barely seems aware of my existence. I should never have come; he never wanted me to in the first place. But at least I know that in a few hours I will be catching the train to Manchester. The thought fills me with a desperate kind of joy.

I walk till the sun is a cold white globe above the skyline. Then I retrace my steps back to the village. My legs are throbbing and I am finally warm by the time I reach the cottage. I check my watch. Only two hours till my train.

Everyone looks at me in surprise. Breakfast is in full swing – Rami eating cereal, Sophie feeding Aurora, Matias buttering toast and Maria hovering with coffee.

'Well, hello!' Maria exclaims.

I collapse on the nearest stool, brushing tangled hair out of my eyes. 'I felt like a walk,' I explain.

They glance behind me, at the still open kitchen door. 'Where's Flynn?' Rami asks me.

'Oh – I went for a walk on my own,' I say, suddenly flustered.

'Good thinking,' Sophie says. 'Come on, Rami, we should take Aurora out after breakfast and try and work off some of this food!'

'You'll have to wrap her up, it's freezing,' I say, gratefully accepting a cup of coffee from Maria.

'Should somebody wake Flynn?' Matias asks.

I look at my watch. It is nearly ten o'clock. I doubt he is sleeping – mooching more like. I put down my coffee. 'I'll go and get him.'

'Flynn!' I throw open the bedroom door. He is still lying in bed, fast asleep, sunlight pouring through the thin curtains. I hesitate, wondering whether to wake him, then remember my train. 'Hey, sleepy-head.' I sit down on the edge of the bed. Stroke his arm. It's not often that I see him sleep. He looks younger somehow, more vulnerable.

'Flynnie . . .' I give his arm a little shake. Bend down and kiss his cheek. He looks strangely flushed and his skin is hot and sweaty. I straighten up. 'Come on, wake up!' I exclaim. 'We're all having breakfast and I've got to leave in half an hour!'

Nothing. I stare down at him. His eyes are tightly shut, his breathing loud and rasping. A cold hand creeps up and squeezes my chest. I can hear my heart.

I grab him by the shoulders and shake him, hard. 'Flynn!'

His head rolls limply on the pillow. His eyes do not open. His breathing stops for a moment and then starts again, harsh and laboured. I leap away from the bed, a scream building in my throat. As I stumble back, something crunches under my feet. Blister packets, empty blister packets, all over the carpet. I hurl myself out of the bedroom door.

'Help! Call an ambulance! Help!' I scream at the top of my voice.

Rami reaches me on the landing. He is trying to restrain me, trying to pull me round to face him. 'Calm down, calm down. What's happening?'

'No! No!' I yell. 'He's unconscious! Call an ambulance!'

Rami grips me by the shoulders. 'Where? Where is he?'

'In the bedroom – the study!' I scream. 'He's in there!'

Rami lets go of me and runs along to the room. I stumble in after him. Suddenly the small room is very crowded. I can hear the sound of a baby crying.

'Oh God!' a woman's voice is moaning. 'Rami, he's all right – he's all right, isn't he?'

I am on my hands and knees, scrabbling through my coat pockets for my mobile phone. My hands are so clammy that it slips from my grasp.

'Mum, Dad, it's all right, it's under control.' Rami is trying to roll Flynn over onto his side, grunting with the effort. 'Sophie – get them downstairs—'

I key in too many nines and have to find the clear button and try again. Sophie is attempting to get Matias and Maria out of the room. Maria has gone white. Matias sounds panicked. 'What's he done? What's he gone and done?'

'Rami needs space,' Sophie is saying desperately, ushering them out. 'It's under control, but he needs some space. Please come downstairs with me – we need to open the door to the paramedics . . .'

'Emergency services. Which service do you require?' comes the voice over the phone.

'Ambulance,' I say desperately.

'Just putting you through.'

'Emergency ambulance service. What's your name?'

I stutter in reply.

'Your telephone number?'

I give them the number from my mobile.

'Your address?'

'Eight Rose – uh – Rosewood Drive,' I stumble. 'Angmering, West Sussex.'

Rami has got Flynn into the recovery position and is kneeling astride him on the bed, taking his pulse and peering at the back of one of the empty blister packs.

'The ambulance is on its way,' the woman says. 'What's the problem?'

'He's taken an overdose.' My voice sounds weird, as if I am being shaken. 'There are a lot of empty pill packets. He's unconscious.'

'Is he breathing?'

'Yes, I – I think so. Rami, is he breathing?'

'Laboured,' Rami grunts.

I repeat this into the phone.

'Is he lying on his back or on his side?'

'He's – he's on his side, Rami's moved him—'

'The ambulance!' Rami shouts. 'Have they sent out the ambulance?'

'Yes, it's on its way!' I yell back

'And are his airways clear?' the operator asks.

'Yes, I – I think so!'

'Can you read what's on the pill packets? Can you tell me how many pills are missing and what it says on the outside of the packets?' the operator continues.

I squat down and scrabble round on the floor, almost dropping the phone. 'Five, ten, fifteen, twenty, twenty-five, forty – I mean thirty – and then there's two more – forty – and it says fluox— I'll – I'll spell it . . .' My mouth feels as if it has gone numb. I can hardly get the words out.

'Benzodiazepines,' Rami barks. 'Tell her he's taken a massive overdose of benzos and ADs.'

I repeat it into the phone. I can feel the sweat running down my back.

'What dose does it say on the packet?' the woman asks.

'Two milligrams. No, I think it's ten . . .' I am seeing double as I try desperately to read the faint type on the sticky label. 'Yes, ten of diza—'

Rami snatches the mobile away from me. 'Four hundred milligrams of diazepam,' he barks down the phone. 'And six hundred milligrams of fluoxetine. Maybe more. When will the ambulance be here?'

Sophie appears in the doorway. She waits until Rami hangs up. Then she asks, 'Is he stable?' Her voice is eerily calm.

'Pulse fifty, pupils non-responsive,' Rami replies. 'Oh Jesus, Sophie!'

'He's still breathing on his own, Rami. Shall we try and get him downstairs ready for the paramedics?'

'No, it's better not to move him.'

'Right. Just keep tabs on his airways and his pulse. That's all you can do for now.'

The wail of a siren suddenly blasts up from the street below. Sophie disappears. Moments later the bedroom is full of people with walkie-talkies and green overalls, crowding round the bed. Everyone is talking very fast. Flynn's nose and mouth are covered with an oxygen mask and a needle is inserted into his arm and taped down. A blood-pressure cuff is attached to his other arm and a thick white neck brace is fitted around him. Then he is lifted onto some kind of chair and covered with a salmon-pink blanket and strapped into it. On the count of three, they lift the chair and manoeuvre it through the bedroom door, jolting it against the door frame. The chair disappears and the room is suddenly empty. I can hear the paramedics grunting and giving instructions to each other on the staircase outside.

I will myself to move, to run downstairs after them and follow Flynn into the ambulance, but nothing happens. I don't seem to be able to get up from the floor. A few minutes later, the sound of the siren wails into life again, sending blue waves of light crashing through the empty room.

Chapter Eight

JENNAH

Sophie comes in carrying the crying baby, and sits down on the edge of the bed. Her face is pale. 'Jennah, listen. Rami's gone in the ambulance with Flynn, and I'm going to arrange for Maria and Matias to be driven to the hospital by a neighbour. Do you want to go with them? I've got to stay here because of Aurora. Rami says he'll call the moment he has news.'

I shake my head dully. I'm afraid that if I try to stand up, my legs will collapse. I still haven't moved from my position on the floor next to the window. The mobile phone is still at my feet.

'Are you sure?'

I nod.

'OK. I'm just going to pop downstairs and go round to the neighbours. Can you watch Aurora for five minutes while I do that?'

I hold out my arms for the crying baby.

'Jennah, speak to me first – can you watch Aurora while I run next door?'

I force my mouth into motion. 'Yes,' I mumble.

'Yes, I'll look after Aurora. She'll be fine with me.'

Sophie looks at me doubtfully, then lowers Aurora down onto my lap. 'Five minutes,' she says.

She gives my shoulder a squeeze and leaves the room. Moments later I hear the sound of raised voices in the street, slamming car doors and the sound of the engine starting up. I jiggle Aurora against my shoulder as she continues to whimper, and bury my face against her soft, warm body. 'Oh baby, baby, baby,' I chant softly. 'Baby, baby, don't cry. Baby, baby, baby, baby. He's going to be all right, he's going to be all right.'

After a few moments Aurora stops crying and starts pulling my hair, demanding to be played with. I force myself up onto my feet, my knees still shaking, and take her downstairs to the toys in the living room. I can't stop trembling. She chews on the ear of her talking teddy, slavering away happily, jiggling her arms and legs up and down, babbling to herself, unperturbed by the silence of her carer.

Sophie returns, pale and breathless.

I look up at her from the carpet. 'He's going to be OK, isn't he?' My voice sounds strange.

Sophie gives me a dazed look. 'I don't know,' she says.

Aurora starts to whine and the sound sets my teeth on edge. I get up off the floor. 'I'm going upstairs to call my mum,' I say.

The bed is still warm. I pull the duvet over my knees and open my mobile. When I blurt out what has happened, there is a moment of shocked silence. 'You mean he tried to kill himself?' Her voice is shrill with horror. She wants to drive down from Manchester to fetch me. I tell her I'm not going anywhere until I know what's happening to Flynn. She sounds angry although I can't figure out why. I try and explain the situation to her but she doesn't seem to want to understand. 'Who *are* these people?' she keeps on asking. 'What's *wrong* with Flynn?' I know it's only out of concern for me, but she makes me want to scream.

Later, Sophie comes upstairs to tell me that Rami called. There is no news. Flynn is still unconscious. He is in intensive care. She asks me if I want some company, whether I want to come downstairs and have something to eat. I decline and she leaves.

The hours pass. I lose track of time. Eventually I wander downstairs and play listlessly with Aurora while Sophie prepares a meal in the kitchen. I try to keep my mind a blank. Sometime in the afternoon, as dusk creeps across the windows, the phone suddenly starts to ring. Sophie has the blender on and cannot hear from the kitchen. I am playing roll-the-ball with Aurora, and for a moment I sit paralysed, unable to move.

'Hello?'

'Jennah, it's Rami. Flynn's OK. He's in intensive care but he's OK. He's breathing on his own and his heart is strong but they're not expecting him to come round for quite a while. I'm going to bring my parents home now and then I'll take you back to the hospital to see him.'

When they come in, Matias is leaning on Rami's arm. Their faces look ashen. Maria's eyes are glazed. Sophie relieves me of Aurora and puts the kettle on, baby on hip. Rami helps his father into a chair and looks across at me. 'Shall I take you over?'

'Wait.' Sophie puts her hand on his arm. 'Sit down and have a sandwich and a cup of tea before you go anywhere.' She pushes him into a chair and puts the baby on his lap. Then she takes the turkey leftovers out of the fridge and starts carving. 'Everyone must eat,' she says firmly.

I force myself upright and join her at the counter to help. We make a sandwich for each person and then sit round the table, trying to consume them. The silence is deafening. Nobody seems to have the strength to talk.

'Right,' Rami says finally, draining his cup. 'Jennah?'

I get up, grab my bag and follow him to the door. 'Drive carefully,' Sophie calls after us.

We drive to the hospital in silence. Rami's thumbs drum against the steering wheel whenever we stop at a red light. We enter the hospital through the car park and take a lift to the very top floor. As the doors ping closed behind us, Rami looks at me and says, 'There are a lot of wires and monitors, Jen.'

'OK. But he's breathing on his own, right?'

Rami nods.

We follow a long, brightly lit corridor till we reach some double doors at the end. Rami presses a buzzer and a nurse in surgical clothes comes to greet us. We leave our coats and bags in a small room and wash our hands with antiseptic soap before being led down a ward filled with a strong medicinal smell. It is very warm. I try not to look to my left or right. From the edge of my vision I am aware of rows of beds, each surrounded by a plethora of bleeping, sucking, humming machines. And at the centre of each, a human being, hovering on the brink of life.

The nurse breaks away from us and veers off towards a bed on the right. 'Here we are,' Rami says softly. I am vaguely aware of his hand reaching for mine, holding it tight. We approach a bed. The first thing I notice is a shock of blond hair. Flynn's skin is completely white. His lips are stretched out to accommodate a large plastic contraption in his mouth. There are tubes up his nose. Both arms are attached to drips, a crisscrossing of surgical tape securing the plastic tubes in the crook of each elbow. A white sheet is pulled up to his middle. His bare chest is covered with red and blue stickers with wires coming out of them, leading to more bleeping machines.

'You can sit down on the side of the bed,' Rami says to me. 'You can talk to him if you want. He might be able to hear you.'

I perch myself gingerly, muscles clenched, terrified of hurting Flynn or somehow dislodging one of the tubes. Rami moves away to talk to the nurse. I stare at Flynn's lifeless face. His eyelids look as if they have been stuck down. There are purple bruises beneath them. The plastic tube in his mouth makes him look like he is pulling a face. For one crazy moment I expect him to open his eyes and say, 'Ha ha, got you!'

His chest rises and falls steadily. The machines pip and bleep. I reach out slowly and touch his hand. I am relieved to find it warm. I uncurl his fingers gently and close my hand round his. His fingers curl back and for an instant I think he is squeezing my hand. Then I realize it is just the natural position of his fingers. I lean forwards. 'Flynn,' I whisper.

Not a flicker.

'Please wake up,' I say softly. 'We all need you. We're all so worried. We all love you. I love you, Flynn. I don't want—' My eyes fill up. 'I don't want to live without you.'

I don't see how he can possibly hear me. His face is like a waxwork, and I realize suddenly with startling clarity that the body and the person are two different things. Two different entities, somehow fused. The body is the one I am looking at now, attached to all these machines, the heart still struggling to pump, the lungs still struggling to breathe, valiantly fighting to stay alive. The person is another being entirely, the perpetrator of this crime, the one who ruthlessly swallowed forty tablets sometime in the middle of the night, then lay down beside his girlfriend to die. The person tried to kill itself, tried to kill its own body. I understand for the first time why attempted suicide used to be an imprisonable offence. It is, after all, attempted murder. The person against the body. *Look what you've done to yourself!* I want to shout. *How could you be so cruel? Your body didn't deserve to be harmed like this – flooded with poison then stuck with needles and fed with tubes!* The words 'mental illness' suddenly take on a whole new dimension. What kind of illness makes life want to bring about its end? It goes against every natural instinct!

I get up unsteadily and look around for Rami. He is by my side in an instant, his arm round my shoulders. 'It's been a long day,' he says. 'Let's go home and get some rest. We'll come back and see him in the morning.'

'Shouldn't someone stay with him?' I blurt out. 'What if he comes round in the night?'

'We need to get some sleep,' Rami says. 'There's no point in us going under too. The doctor says he'll be out for twenty-four hours at least. All they can do now is monitor him carefully until the drugs work their way through his body.'

Rami goes over to speak to one of the nurses. I hear him ask her to call him on his mobile if there is any change in the night. We leave.

'Why?' I say in the car. 'Why would anyone want to do that to themselves?'

'Mum was asking the same thing,' Rami says, starting the engine. 'Depression is a strange thing. It's dehumanizing, somehow.'

'Is he definitely going to come round?' I ask. 'Are the doctors absolutely sure about that?'

'Once the drugs work their way through his body, they think he'll probably just wake up,' Rami says.

'Probably?' I say.

'Well, there are three possibilities. One is that he'll just wake up feeling groggy but fine,' he explains. 'The other possibility is that he'll need a liver transplant, although so far tests show that his liver is labouring, but coping.'

'And the third possibility?' I ask, my heart in my mouth.

Rami exhales slowly. 'With any prolonged state of unconsciousness, there is always the risk of brain-damage,' he says. 'But there's no way of knowing until he wakes up.'

I stare straight ahead. A fine rain begins to fall. The lights of passing cars are refracted through the pattern of raindrops across the windscreen. Rami switches on the wipers. It is Boxing Day and the streets are still empty.

I sleep in fits and starts in the squeaky, empty bed, haunted by fragments of dreams. Finally I emerge hot and sweaty from the duvet and sit cross-legged in the middle of the bed, the window open, a mini-gale buffeting around me, my body aching from the cold. I watch a weak dawn rise above the rooftops and I wonder whether Flynn is still breathing. I imagine the doctor coming down the long hospital corridor towards us to tell us that Flynn has died in the night. I imagine Maria collapsing. I try to think of what to say – of what to say to Rami, to Matias, to Maria. I fail.

Rami takes Maria and Matias to the hospital after breakfast. I stay with Sophie and the baby since there is no point in us all being there at once. I have hardly seen Matias and Maria since all this happened. They look broken, like ghosts of their previous selves. I feel like running into the hospital and shaking Flynn awake – *Look what you have done to your parents!* I want to shout. *Look what you have done to us all!*

I feed Aurora while Sophie makes the coffee. As I am scooping up dribbles of food from Aurora's chin, Sophie passes behind me and rubs my arm. I say nothing and continue to feed the baby, breathing deeply against the threat of tears.

Rami brings Matias and Maria back late morning. They look totally spent. I help Sophie make lunch. In the afternoon, Sophie insists Rami stays at home with Aurora while she drives me to the hospital. Again I sit on the edge of Flynn's hospital bed and reach for his inert hand. His face is still sealed shut. There is a different nurse hovering nearby, and bright winter sunlight streams through the windows. 'It's a beautiful day,' I tell him. 'The sun is really strong and the sky is bright blue.' I tentatively squeeze his hand. His eyelashes do not move.

That evening, Rami goes back to the hospital with his parents. We seem to have fallen into some kind of a routine. Harry calls me on my mobile. He wants to know where Flynn is – they were supposed to meet this evening to practise their composition piece, but he hasn't shown up. I tell him what has happened.

'God, no!' Harry breathes. 'Do you want me to come down, Jen? Is – is he allowed visitors?'

I tell him there is no point, that Flynn is unconscious. Harry sounds deeply shocked. I promise to call him as soon as there is more news. Sophie and I spend the afternoon watching re-runs of *Friends.* Neither of us smile, but the sound of canned laughter reminds me that life somehow goes on.

The following day, a similar routine unfolds. Rami takes his parents to the hospital first thing, while Sophie, Aurora and I go to the supermarket. It is a relief to be doing something useful. After picking at our lunch, Sophie and I drive over to the hospital. Flynn still looks exactly the same. Sophie leans over him and strokes his cheek and says some words in his ear. I just want to leave.

In the car on the way home, I am jolted out of my stupor by Sophie lifting her hand off the steering wheel to wipe her eyes. I turn to her in panic. 'Soph—'

Her cheeks flush slightly and she sniffs hard and shakes her head with a smile. 'I'm just being silly. I know he's going to be fine,' she says quickly.

I gaze at her silently, wondering why she is the one crying and not me.

'Oh, Jennah, I'm sorry. I'm just going to pull over for

a minute so I don't get back to the house looking a complete mess . . .' She slows the car to a halt at the top of the lane and rummages around in the glove box for a tissue. She finds a crumpled one and presses it quickly to her eyes. 'This is what broken nights with an eight-month-old reduce one to!' She laughs through the tears.

'You're really fond of him, aren't you,' I say. My heart hurts.

'Well, he's the only brother-in-law I've got, so I'd rather hang onto him if at all possible!' Sophie replies.

'Do you think he's going to die?' I ask. The tone of my voice makes it sound like I'm asking her whether it's going to rain.

Sophie looks at me quickly. 'Oh no, Jen, I don't. I think he's going to be fine.'

The next day is Friday. I can't believe that Christmas Day was only four days ago. It seems like a lifetime. We have entered some kind of twilight zone, our waking hours divided between the cottage and the hospital. Mum calls to ask for news. She sounds worried and begs me to come home. I struggle not to raise my voice. Later Harry calls, then Kate. It seems like a terrible effort to talk, just to tell them there is no change.

On Friday night I am pulled from a splintered sleep by a gentle but persistent knocking on the bedroom door. Rami is on the landing, buttoning his shirt, his hair dishevelled. My heart leaps into my throat and I let out a strangled cry.

'It's all right!' His hands grip my arms, pushing me back into the room. 'Shh, shh, I don't want to wake the others. One of the nurses called. They say he's coming round. Do you want to come with me to the hospital?'

'Yes! Of course!'

'Get dressed then.'

I grab my jeans from the chair and stumble into them, pull on a jumper and shove on my shoes. Rami is waiting by the front door, jangling the keys in his hand. It is freezing in the car. I shiver all the way to the hospital. The luminous digits on the radio read 3:04 a.m. We hurry through the empty, brightly lit corridors, now all too familiar. A nurse I recognize lets us into the intensive care ward with a big smile. After going through the prerequisite hand-washing, we are led over to Flynn's bed. I can feel my heart.

'He's groggy,' the nurse tells us, 'but he knows where he is.'

I freeze at the sight of him, sitting propped up against the pillows. Rami keeps going and I watch him approach Flynn's bedside and mime a slow-motion punch to his brother's head. He sits down on the edge of the bed and leans forwards. I can't hear what he is saying. I seem to be unable to move. I cannot believe that Flynn is back. The inert, sealed, waxwork body is gone. Now, his eyes are open and he is sitting up, talking, moving. The tube in his mouth has been removed, and his hair is all on end. Someone touches my arm. It's the nurse. 'Come and sit down,' she says.

She leads me to a chair against the wall. I can't see Flynn's bed from here. I rest my elbows on my knees and try to slow my breathing. The nurse smiles down at me kindly. 'Would you like a drink of water?'

I shake my head. Wipe my wet palms against my jeans.

'Stay sitting for a little while,' the nurse says. 'I'll bring you some water in case you change your mind.'

She moves off and I sit up, taking a deep breath and letting it out slowly. I clench my teeth and stare at the humming machinery surrounding another patient's bed in front of me. The strong artificial lights seem to be throbbing all around. I feel like I'm losing my mind.

The nurse brings me a paper cup of water and I take it from her, my hand shaking. I sip it and stare hard at the tips of my shoes, trying to focus my mind. Sometime later Rami comes up to me, looking concerned. 'The nurse said you weren't feeling too well,' he says, his hand on my arm. 'Do you need to get some fresh air?'

I dig my nails painfully into the palm of my hand. 'I'm fine,' I say thickly.

'Do you want to go and see him?' Rami asks.

I nod.

'I'm going to grab myself a coffee, then. I'll meet you at the car.'

I nod again. Stand up slowly. Rami gives me a pat on

the back, then turns to wave at Flynn before setting off down the ward. I want to scream at him to come back.

As I approach Flynn's bed, he looks up and gives me a tired smile.

'Hi.' I kiss him quickly on the cheek and sit down on the edge of the bed. He smells of medicine and sweat. There are sticky marks on his chest where the red and blue stickers were. He is down to just one drip. The crook of his other arm is bruised purple and yellow. His lips are raw and cracked. His hair looks in bad need of a wash. His eyes seem to take a long time to focus. I bite my lip, hard.

He lifts one hand off the sheet. Touches my cheek clumsily. 'Hello,' he says hoarsely.

I swallow what feels like a golf ball in my throat. 'You gave us quite a scare,' I say with difficulty.

He blinks. Nods slowly. 'Yeah, Rami was saying . . .'

My fists are clenched so tight, my fingers feel like they are going to break. 'Your – your mum and dad will be delighted to see you finally awake.'

He nods again. 'Yeah.'

I take a desperate breath and look around. 'Looks like they've taken you off most of the machines,' I say stupidly.

He raises the arm still attached to the drip. 'This, apparently, is saline. I don't really see why I can't just drink a couple of glasses of water instead.' He shifts his leg under the sheet. 'And I've got a tube in here so I don't even have to get up to pee.' He smiles again slowly.

I feel like I'm falling, yet I'm still sitting on the side of the bed. 'How – how are you feeling?'

'Sleepy and thirsty. My mouth feels like sandpaper, but they won't let me drink.'

'Why not?'

'Don't know. Something about being sick. But they said they'd take the last tubes out tomorrow.'

He turns his head slightly on the pillow as a nurse approaches. 'Hello, this is my girlfriend, Jennah,' he says.

I stand up.

'It's fine, don't move,' the nurse says to me with a big smile. She turns to Flynn. 'I'm just going to take your blood pressure.'

I back away. 'I'd – I'd better go now. Rami's waiting for me downstairs.'

Flynn's smile fades. 'Will you come back tomorrow?'

'Yes, of course.' I raise my hand and wave goodbye. Then I turn and hurry out of the ward.

I reach the Ford in the freezing car park only to find it locked and Rami nowhere around.

'Bloody hell!' I exclaim, and suddenly find myself savagely kicking the door. I'm fighting with the handle, tears blinding me. I hear someone shout my name. I break into a run. I exit the car park and career down the street, the sobs threatening to choke me. I can hear the pounding of feet on the pavement behind me.

'Jennah, wait!'

I run blindly across the road and a car blares its horn.

I head up a dark country lane, my sobbing breath exploding into the still night air.

'Jennah, for God's sake!' Rami is behind me. He catches me by the wrist and pulls me round. 'Stop, stop, calm down—'

'Let go of me!' I scream, struggling with all my might.

'Not until you calm down.' He has my wrist in a vice-like grip. I crumple to the ground, sobbing wildly. He squats down beside me. 'Jennah, what – what – tell me—'

'I hate him!' I scream.

'Who, Flynn?'

'Yes! I h-hate him! I wished he had died if that's what he wanted! I hate him!'

'I know,' Rami says.

'No, you d-don't!' I sob. 'I hate him! I don't love him! I hate him!'

'One can both love and hate someone, Jen.'

'I don't *want* to love him!' I start to cry really hard. 'I don't want to love him, Rami! I don't want to!'

'I know,' Rami says.

I put my hands over my face. 'I can't do this, I can't do this any more. It's too hard!'

Rami's strokes my back as I rock back and forth, sobbing into my hands. 'What am I supposed to do! I just don't know what to do! I try to help him, I t-try! But it doesn't make any difference! He still hates his life, he still wants to die!'

'He doesn't always want to die,' Rami says.

'But it's going to keep coming back! The depression's going to keep coming back! He'll try again. And what if he succeeds? What if next time he succeeds?' I burst into renewed sobs.

'He might not succeed,' Rami says. 'He might not even try again.'

'But what if he does?' I yell through my hands.

'Um, excuse me . . .' I hear a man's voice.

'She's all right,' Rami says. 'She's with me. She's my friend. She's just a bit upset.'

I feel a hand on my shoulder. 'Are you all right, miss?'

I drag my hands away from my face and look up into an unfamiliar bearded face. 'Do you know this man?' the stranger asks me.

'Y-yes,' I gasp.

'That's all right then.' He pats me on the shoulder. 'There's a hospital just down the road if you need help,' I hear him tell Rami.

'Thanks,' Rami replies.

I press my fingers against my wet cheeks and take a few shuddering breaths.

'I guess it doesn't look too good, me wrestling on the pavement with a screaming girl,' Rami says, a smile in his voice.

I sniff hard, the sobs beginning to die down.

'Here . . .' He presses some tissues into my hand.

I am suddenly aware of the cold and damp seeping into the seat of my jeans. I am freezing. I drag the tissues across my cheeks, blow my nose.

'I'm sorry,' I say quietly.

'You have nothing to be sorry about,' Rami says. 'Nothing. Do you understand?'

I nod, exhausted. Rami stands up and holds out his hand. 'Come on, let's go home,' he says.

Chapter Nine

FLYNN

The day after I come round, they transfer me out of the ICU and into a normal ward, where they keep me hooked up to a heart monitor. I sleep a lot even though the ward is really noisy and the nurses keep waking me up to take my blood pressure. After a few days, I am taken into a small room with two doctors and a social worker and asked a whole barrage of questions about the overdose. Later I find out I am being moved to another hospital. All the tubes are out and I'm bored out of my mind from lying in bed all day, but they say that I can't go home. The place I'm going to is a psychiatric hospital near Brighton, twelve miles away. I say, 'You've got to be joking,' and they reply, 'I'm afraid you don't have a choice.' Then Rami comes to speak to me and tells me it will be easier if I just go along with it. I try not to get too visibly upset because Rami looks exhausted. Anyway, this is all just stupid bureaucracy. I'll be able to slip away easily enough when I get to this new place. I am perfectly sure the NHS has better things to do than run after me.

A woman and a man come to pick me up around noon. They introduce themselves as Sue and Ash. Sue has multicoloured hair and Ash is as camp as they come. Sue drives and Ash gets into the back seat beside me. Rami and my parents are supposed to be meeting me at the new hospital with some of my clothes and stuff. As if they expect me to stay there! What a fuss.

When I arrive outside the formidable white-pillared stone building, set back from the winding country lane in acres of parkland, things don't exactly go to plan. I expected to find Rami and my parents waiting outside, ready to be persuaded to drive me home. Jennah and I would then catch the 16.23 from Angmering station and be back in London in time for dinner. But there is nobody waiting for me when I arrive and Ash doesn't leave my side.

I am taken into a sort of waiting room and I have to fill in lots of forms and hand over all my 'personal possessions'. I have nothing visible on me except for my mobile phone and my watch. But they ask for my belt as well, then my shoes. I am annoyed – it's going to be a pain trying to retrieve all this stuff once my parents arrive. When they insist on seeing the contents of my pockets, I feel my blood pressure begin to rise. They take the coins and the bunch of keys. They put it all in an envelope with my name. Then they make me follow them upstairs in my socks.

There is a heavy-duty fireproof door on the first landing, and Sue pulls out a card and swipes it through a slot and a buzzer sounds and the door is pushed open. I stop, but Ash, coming up close behind me, pushes me on through. As the door clicks shut behind us, I turn, looking back the way we came. Suddenly I can feel my heart.

'Why are these doors locked? This isn't a prison, for Christ's sake!'

'This way . . .' Ash's hand is on my shoulder. I shrug him off angrily.

Sue leads us down a long corridor, then up some more stairs, then through another card-operated door and down another corridor. There are lime-green doors down either side, most of them open or ajar. Music plays from one room, people sitting on a bed. Canned laughter from a TV. Someone comes careering down the corridor, shouting at the top of their voice. We squeeze aside. I am shown a kitchen, a communal room, a shower room, another kitchen. Then Sue stops outside a closed door and sifts through a large bunch of keys before unlocking it. A bedroom. Thin brown carpet, faded wallpaper. A window with bars over it, painted the same lime-green. A small bed. A small desk. A desk lamp, a chair.

'This is your room, Flynn. We'll bring your stuff up and then you can get settled. Doctor Rasheed is one of our resident psychiatrists and you have an appointment with her tomorrow morning at eleven o'clock. There is a timetable on your desk – there's a group meeting this afternoon at four o'clock, when you'll be introduced to the others.' She begins to move away.

'Wait,' I say desperately. 'Where are my brother and my parents? They were supposed to bring me my clothes and—'

'A suitcase has been left for you in reception,' Sue says. 'I'll get someone to bring it up. Your brother dropped it off earlier—'

'No, hold on, they were supposed to wait for me!' I can't believe what I'm hearing.

'Your brother said he'd be back with your parents to see you tomorrow once you'd settled in,' Sue says matter-of-factly.

'I'm not spending the night here! They were supposed to come and pick me up! Give me back my stuff. I'm leaving.'

Sue looks at me calmly. 'Flynn, you are being detained under section two of the nineteen eighty-four Mental Health Act. Until you're better, you'll be staying here.' She hands me some kind of leaflet. 'This outlines your rights. Have a read through it and if you have any questions, don't hesitate to ask.'

The blood begins to pound in my ears. This can't be happening. I am being sectioned, locked up in a psychiatric hospital against my will, forced by law to remain here until I am deemed fit to return to general society. I stare at her, breathing hard. 'Is there a phone I can use?'

'There's a pay phone at the end of the hall,' Sue says. 'You'll need to ask for a phone card at the nurses' station.' She moves to the door. 'I'll go and see if I can find your suitcase now.'

I sit down on the edge of the sagging bed, trying not to panic. A cold film of sweat has broken out across my back. I stand up and look around me, a feeling of despair mounting in my throat. I leave the room and go down to a door marked NURSES' STATION, where Ash and some other people with name-badges stand about drinking coffee and listening to the radio. I ask for a phone card. It all takes ages. When I finally get to the pay phone and start dialling, my hands are shaking.

'Hello?'

'Rami, is that you?'

'Yeah, have you arrived?'

'Yes. What the hell's going on? Come and fetch me.'

'I can't, Flynn.' His voice is surprisingly firm.

'I'll just leave then. No one's going to keep me here against my will.' I am trying to keep my voice down, acutely aware of some of the other patients milling around curiously. I turn to face the wall.

'Flynn, listen to me. Give the place a chance. They have some very good psychiatrists and you need to be in a residential unit right now.'

I press my fist against my mouth and bite my knuckles to keep from screaming. 'I'll just walk out then,' I say raggedly. 'If you can't be fucking bothered to come and fetch me, I'll just walk home.'

'Flynn, don't do that. They'll just fetch you back. You're not well enough to be living on your own right now. Listen, you're in a good hospital. I have a feeling they are really going to be able to help you—'

I punch the wall. 'Bloody hell, Rami! Come and get me now!' I shout.

There are titters behind me.

'Put Dad on the phone!' I command.

There is a pause. I hear the sound of muffled talking in the background. Then Dad's voice. 'Flynn?'

'Dad, I'm not staying here—'

'Flynn, we love you very much but we want you to get better,' Dad says in a rush. 'We'll come and see you tomorrow, OK? I'm going to hand you back to Rami now.'

'Dad!' I yell.

Rami comes back on the line. 'It's going to be all right, Flynn. Just give the place a chance.'

'Put Jennah on the phone!'

'Jennah's not here, Flynn. She's gone to her mother's—'

I slam the receiver down with all my strength. My chest feels as if it's going to burst.

'Hey, dude, have a fag and chill!' someone says.

I knock the hand away, stride down the corridor and bang into my bedroom. I look wildly for a lock, and end up sitting on the floor with my back against the door. The sobs tear at my throat. Who would have thought forty pills wouldn't be enough?

I don't go to their 'group meeting'. Someone comes in and tries to persuade me but I keep my head in my arms until they go away. I don't go to dinner either. If I refuse to eat, they will be forced to release me. But the real reason is that I can't stop crying. I'm so tired. I'm so tired of everything. This is worse than being depressed. This is worse than anything imaginable.

After a while I pull myself up from the hard floor and crawl up onto the bed. Later, someone comes in and leaves a sandwich on a plate. At some point I fall asleep. The next thing I am aware of is being shaken awake by one of the nurses. She hands me three tablets and a plastic cup of water. Fucking lithium. I contemplate throwing the water in her face but then decide it is too much effort. I swallow the pills. I only wish I could swallow a couple of handfuls more.

'There's a bathroom just across the corridor. You need to get ready for bed now,' she says. 'Lights go off in twenty minutes.'

I glare at her. 'I think I'm old enough to go to bed when I want to,' I say acidly.

She shrugs as if to say, *It's all the same to me*, and leaves the room.

I lie back down and get under the duvet because I am cold. The bed smells rank. Sometime later someone comes in and switches off the light. My door is left ajar. There is a light on at the end of the corridor. I can hear laughter from the room next door. I get up and cross the corridor. Chatting and music waft out from the nurses' station. Someone calls out, 'Hey, Stu, what are you doing in Nina's bed?' followed by raucous laughter.

I pee in the crappy bathroom with no lock, then go back to bed, kicking my door closed. Moments later it opens again. I pull the duvet over my head and try to sleep.

Two hours later I am ready to pull my hair out. I am hot and sweaty, the bed still smells and I am about as far from sleep as possible. I get up, pull on my jeans and leave my room. There is nowhere to go. I start to pace the dimly lit corridor. Someone is snoring. Someone else is singing. I start counting the lengths of the corridor. When I reach length twenty-four, Ash appears from the nurses' station and tells me I need to try to sleep. I ignore him and just keep on walking. When I reach length eighty-two, Sue comes out of the nurses' station and asks me if I want a sleeping pill. I ignore her too. I reach the hundreds before I start to lose count. I am seeing double. When I snag my toe in the carpet and sprawl onto the floor, I can't be bothered to get up. At some point I am dimly aware of being walked back to my bed.

The next day, after breakfast, I see the psychiatrist, a Dr Rasheed. She is a po-faced woman who spends the whole hour asking me about my childhood and writing lengthy notes. Afterwards I am forced to attend 'group' – a bunch of people from my 'unit' sitting around in the common room. There are six of us on this floor – a punk girl with a lot of body-piercing, a long-haired teenage boy, a girl with scars all down her arms, a guy who must be over twenty stone and a girl who is barely more than a skeleton. When I am asked to introduce myself, I say, 'I'm Flynn.' I am asked if I want to expand, I say, 'No.' The session consists primarily of everyone bitching about the rules, complaining about the food and demanding more cigarette-outings. I spend the time staring down at my feet.

'Visiting time' happens in the common room on the floor below. We sit on a small cluster of plastic chairs, trying to shut out all the other voices. Dad has difficulty meeting my eyes. Mum looks pale. Rami is all positive and full of brotherly cheer. I want to hit him. When I ask how long I have to be here for, he says he doesn't know. I start to swear at him, and Mum gets flustered. Dad excuses himself and walks out of the room. I leave soon after. I know Mum is going to cry, but I don't care, I honestly don't care. I hate them all.

That evening, after a disgusting dinner of bangers and mash, I screw up the courage – or perhaps it is simply the desperation – to call Jennah. I dial her mum's number, then sit down cross-legged, facing the wall.

When she comes on the line, she sounds uncertain, hesitant.

'Hey! Guess where I am?' I ask, my voice loud with false cheer.

'Rami told me. The Wellesley Hospital in Worthing. What's it like?'

'For a loony-bin it's actually quite decent,' I reply. 'I don't have Sky or an en-suite, and the menu isn't exactly à la carte, but you know . . .' I tail off.

There is a silence. 'Do you have your own room?' Jennah asks.

'Oh yeah, yeah. I have a lovely view of the sea from between the bars of my window.'

She doesn't laugh. 'Have you started' – there is a pause as she searches for the right word – 'treatment?'

'Yeah, yeah. We had group therapy today. Tomorrow we'll probably have art therapy – maybe I'll draw you a house and a garden. I know, perhaps they'll teach us to make baskets! Isn't that why they call us basket cases?'

'Flynn, stop,' Jennah softly implores.

'And we'll probably have music therapy the day after. Maybe I'll get to play the tambourine. Or the triangle. I've always wanted to play the triangle!'

'Flynn—'

'No, I'm serious! I'll ask for some manuscript paper and see if I can write a composition for tambourine and triangle. Then I can post it off to you to hand in for my next composition assignment.'

'Flynn, listen—'

'Hold on, hold on! I'm making a note to myself now: *Find fellow insane musician and start composing the Flynn Laukonen Sonata for Tambourine and Triangle.*'

'Flynn—'

'And then, when they let me out, if they ever let me out, perhaps you could pull a few strings and organize for me and my tambourine buddy to give a recital. I'm not sure where though – how about the subway at Marble Arch tube? Nice and central, good acoustics—'

'What are the other people like?' Jennah cuts in, an edge to her voice. I notice she doesn't use the word *patients.* Clever Jennah. For a moment there you almost made me forget I was locked up in a mental institution.

'Round the bend, just like me,' I reply. 'I'm in excellent company. We'll be swapping suicide tips in no time at all!' I give a harsh laugh.

There is a silence.

'Flynn, I'm going to go.'

My heart skips a beat. 'Jennah – wait – don't—'

Silence.

'Jennah?' I shout without meaning to. My voice catches in my throat.

'I'm here.'

I close my eyes and rest my forehead against the wall. I can't speak.

'You're such a silly,' she says.

I hold my breath and press my hand against my eyes.

'I miss you so much, you know.'

I sink my teeth into the side of my thumb.

'Flynn, are you still there?'

'Mm.'

'Describe your surroundings to me,' she says. 'I want to be able to close my eyes and see you.'

I cannot reply.

'Flynn?' she says softly. 'I'm looking at the moon. Can you see it too?'

I drag my sleeve over my cheeks and heave for breath.

'Oh, Flynn,' Jennah says.

There is another long silence during which I try unsuccessfully to stem the tears.

'D'you want to call me back later?' Jennah asks.

'No,' I gasp.

'OK. Well then, shall I tell you about my day?'

' 'Kay.'

Jennah launches into a description of her train journey up to Manchester, complete with wrong platforms and missing tickets. I don't know if she is elaborating just for my benefit, but I am grateful. I sit there, the phone glued to my ear, clawing at my cheeks, trying to pull myself together, a task not made any easier by the sound of her voice.

'Jennah?' I say eventually.

'Yes?'

'Are you going to come and see me?'

'Of course I am. I'm going back to the flat on Saturday night, and so I'll pack up some of your stuff and take the train down on Sunday.'

Sunday is six days away. I won't survive.

'Jennah?'

'Yes?'

'I'm really sorry!'

'You don't need to be sorry. Just concentrate on getting better. That's all I want, Flynn. Try your hardest, my love, just try.'

* * *

Back in my bedroom, I turn off the light and lie on the bed, staring up at my small barred window. If I close one eye slightly, I think I can make out the moon.

Chapter Ten

JENNAH

My mother is doing my head in. I crumbled as soon as I saw her and ended up telling her all about Flynn and the bipolar disorder on our way back in the car. When we got home, Alan went out to give us some space, and Mum and I had dinner together and talked well into the night. For once she just listened. I could see the shock growing in her eyes, as well as the look of hurt that I had kept so much from her. We went to bed in the small hours of the morning and I slept for a very long time. When I awoke, it was three in the afternoon and almost dark again. But Mum looked as if she hadn't been to bed at all. 'Just tell me one thing,' she said to me, her voice low and scared. 'Has he ever been violent?'

I wasn't sure how to answer that question. I didn't know if she meant violent towards me or just violent in general. My hesitation was a big mistake.

She hasn't left the topic alone since. 'Bipolar disorder is a very serious illness,' she informs me the following morning as she sits in front of the computer in her little makeshift office at the end of the kitchen.

'It says here that bipolar disorder tends to run in families, and there is strong evidence that it is inherited.'

God, she is so transparent.

'I'm not exactly trying to get pregnant,' I point out acidly, pouring cereal into a bowl.

'And it says here that people with bipolar disorder will spend as much as a quarter of their adult lives in hospital, and a quarter of their adult lives disabled,' Mum continues, ignoring me. 'Have you done any research on the Internet? Some of these facts are really quite sobering.'

I say nothing and pour milk forcefully into my bowl, sloshing some onto the table.

'And did you know that one in five patients with bipolar disorder actually succeeds in committing suicide?' Mum asks, in a voice that would be more suited to describing the weather.

'Oh for God's sake!' I slap my spoon down onto the table.

Mum looks over at me, all bewildered and surprised. 'I just thought you might be interested to know, Jennah. There seem to be an awful lot of websites about it. Shall I print some of this out for you?'

'No!' I exclaim. 'God, what's the matter with you?'

She gives me a hurt look. 'I just want you to be *aware.* For example, did you know that children of a parent with bipolar have a thirty per cent chance of inheriting the disorder?'

'Fine!' I snap. 'What are you trying to say? That I should just break up with him?'

Mum gives me another of her pained looks, making me feel like the unreasonable child that I am. 'No,' she says quietly. 'I just want you to know what you're letting yourself in for.'

'Well, thank you very much, now I know,' I retort. 'Can we talk about something else?'

'Of course we can. But, Jennah, I really think you should do some research into this. There are a lot of very good sites. This one here has a question and answer section. Shall I print it out for you?'

'Mum, no!'

'Look, this is interesting,' she goes on as if she hasn't heard me. 'It says here that lithium has a response rate of only forty to fifty per cent.'

I take a deep breath to counteract the urge to scream. 'Mum, please! Just stop it!'

'Jennah, I just—'

'Yes, yes, I know.' I cut her off at the pass. 'You just want me to be aware. Well, guess what, I *am* aware! I do have the Internet at home, you know!'

'Yes, but have you really thought about it? Have you really thought about how this could affect the whole of your future, the rest of your life?'

'Mum, as far as I know, Flynn hasn't proposed!'

'Yes, but can't you see the path you're on? You're *living* together now; it's not just some piddly school thing. And the longer you're in this relationship, the harder it's going to be to extract yourself, especially if he has suicidal tendencies—'

'Oh my God!' I want to tear out my hair. I've tried shouting, I wonder if crying would help. 'So what do you want me to do?'

'I just want you to think!'

'I *have* thought!' I shout. 'I've thought and thought. Basically, what it boils down to is that I have only two options. To stay with him or to break up with him. Do you agree?'

'Jennah, you really—'

'Can you see a third option?' I shout. 'What's the third option then? Tell me, tell me!'

'Jennah, stop being so belligerent.' Mum is pulling her downtrodden-mother act now. I want to hit her.

I try to lower my voice a fraction. 'Mum, really, I would love to hear a third option. Please tell me what it is.'

'Well, I don't really think there is one.'

'Thank you,' I say angrily. 'So out of the two available options – stay with him or break up with him – which one do you think I should choose?'

'Well, if you put it like that' – Mum refuses to be mollified – 'I suppose I would say you have to think of yourself, of your future, of what you want. If someday you might want a family—'

'So basically you're saying I should break up with him.'

'Well, not necessarily.' She tries to back out.

'So you're saying I should stay with him then?' I goad her.

'No!' she exclaims vehemently. 'Not unless you're prepared to live like this – with suicide attempts and hospitalizations and the risk of having children with the same illness and going through the whole cycle again with them.'

I knead my head in exasperation. 'Mum, stop beating about the bush. You're basically saying I should break up with him, aren't you?'

Mum gives me a long look. 'I just want my daughter to be happy,' she says quietly. 'I want her to have a partner who is stable and able to hold down a job and provide her with the emotional security and companionship that I never had.'

I drop my head onto my folded arms. In her own infuriating way, she has given me her answer.

On Saturday I take the train back to London, armed with a sheaf of Internet printouts, courtesy of my mother. I figured it was easier to just take them than to argue. When I get back to the flat and unpack my rucksack, I stuff the wad of pages into a drawer without even glancing at them. It's not as if I haven't looked up this stuff already. But I refuse to reduce my relationship with Flynn to a list of statistics and start playing devil's advocate. We just don't know what is going to happen in the future, no matter what the statisticians have to say.

I grab a holdall from the top of the wardrobe and

start gathering some of Flynn's things together. I can't find any clean jeans so I put a wash on. I find myself packing the bag with the care of a mother sending her child to holiday camp. I look around the flat to see what else he might need. Some books, his iPod, his mobile phone charger, the Rachmaninov score he is working on at the moment. Rami has already been by to pick up the laptop and the keyboard. I feel as if I should bake – something homemade, something personal. Only problem is, I'm not much of a cook. I pick up the phone and dial Harry's number to ask if he's got a recipe. He says he'll drive round and bring me his cookbook. While I am waiting for him to arrive, I pop out to the supermarket and do a quick shop.

Harry arrives while I am putting the food away. He gives me a hug and says, 'Happy New Year.'

'Well, it can only get better,' I say with a wry smile.

I leaf through Harry's cookbook and choose a recipe for brownies that doesn't look too labour-intensive. Harry tells me about his Christmas with Kate and her family while I crack eggs into a bowl. He then asks me more about Flynn's hospitalization and I fill him in. He looks grave. 'So I guess the lithium's just not working for him any more.'

'Well, according to my mother, lithium only works for forty per cent of sufferers,' I reply.

Harry winces. 'You told her?'

'Had to.'

'What was the reaction?'

'Not good. She's as worried as hell. Tried to scare me off with the hundred and one most depressing facts about bipolar disorder. I think she's terrified he's going to turn out to be a violent bastard like my father was.'

Harry gives me a look. 'And what do you think?'

'I don't know.' For a moment I am at a loss. 'I don't want to break up with him. I love him. It seems so stupid, to finally find someone who you really care about, only to let them go.' I look at him. 'Would you break up with Kate if she had a mental illness?'

Harry hesitates. 'I would like to think not,' he says. 'But the reality – the reality could be different. I mean, living with the illness on a day-to-day basis . . .' He tapers off. 'But God, Jen, if you broke up with him—' He stops suddenly.

'What?' I demand, sifting flour into a bowl.

Harry looks uneasy. 'He would – well, it would be hard on him, that's all.'

'It would be hard on me too,' I point out.

'Yeah, but Flynn's – you know – artistic temperament and all that.'

'I'm not going to break up with him,' I say. 'I don't want to break up with him. I love him. That's all that really matters.'

Harry looks relieved. 'Yeah. You two will find a way through all this, I'm sure.'

The following afternoon, after an hour's train ride and a fifteen-minute taxi ride, I arrive outside the huge white-pillared hospital and walk up the gravel driveway. At the reception desk I am asked to sign in, then I'm given a sticky label to wear. I sit on a posh upholstered sofa in a pleasant waiting room overlooking the lawns. The receptionist makes a phone call, and a few minutes later a middle-aged guy with a goatee and an earring comes in.

'Hi, I'm Ash,' he says. 'You're here to see Flynn Laukonen?'

'Yes.' I stand up quickly.

'OK, well, I can take you up, although I should warn you that Flynn's not very well at the moment.'

I stare at him. What the hell does he mean?

'Can I see him?' I ask, my heart beginning to pound.

'Of course,' Ash replies. He turns and leads me up several staircases and along various corridors. The doors at the end of each corridor are thick and heavy and opened with a swipe card.

At the end of a particularly noisy corridor, Ash stops in a doorway. 'Flynn, your friend is here to see you.' He has to shout to make himself heard. The sound of the television, music and laughter erupt from within. Ash steps back. 'Go on through,' he says to me. 'I'll be in the nurses' station at the end of the corridor if you need to have a word.'

Ash departs and I enter the room. It is a small common room with low-slung chairs, a coffee table, a threadbare brown carpet and a television. Half a dozen people are sitting around, some on the chairs, others on the floor. One woman is a punk, with heavily tattooed arms and piercings on various parts of her face. One guy has acne-ridden skin and gazes out from behind a curtain of greasy hair. Flynn is sitting on the arm of the sofa, strumming a guitar. I stand in shock.

'Hey!' The greasy-haired boy is the first to notice me. 'Are you an agency nurse? What's your name?'

Flynn looks up and practically drops his guitar. 'Holy shit!' he exclaims loudly.

I can feel my heart.

'What? What's going on? Who the hell is she?' Punk Lady asks, turning from the television.

Flynn throws down the guitar and leaps up. 'Hey, look, everyone, this is Jennah! The wonderful, beautiful, incredibly talented Jennah!' He grabs me by the waist and swings me around. 'I told you she'd come, didn't I? Didn't I? You didn't believe me, Stu, you arsehole.' He lets go of me abruptly and starts to pummel the boy with the hair.

I stumble back, my face hot with embarrassment.

'Hey, you weren't lying, Piano Boy!' someone shouts. 'She *is* pretty!'

I feel like I'm going to pass out. I try and back out of the door but Flynn grabs me by the arm. 'Jennah, Jennah, meet Stu and Nina and Roz and Naz and Dino!'

'Hi.' I give them a quick smile and try to drag Flynn out into the corridor after me, but he resists, strongly. 'Wait, wait, where are you going? We want to show you what we're doing! Can you guess what we're doing? Can you? Can you?' The colour is high in his cheeks. His eyes are alight.

'Flynn,' I whisper desperately. 'Let's just go somewhere quiet where we can talk . . .'

He ignores me and drags me back into the room by my arm. 'OK, Jennah, sit down, sit down. Stu, get off that bloody chair, you oaf, and let her sit down.' He grabs the guitar. 'OK. Ready? Ready? Naz, are you paying attention?' He clicks his fingers repeatedly in front of the poor girl's face, then begins to strum the guitar. There are a few embarrassed titters from the others, but Flynn stares them down and counts them in. People start singing. Oh, dear God. Someone is playing the recorder. Another has some kind of African drum. Long Hair and Punk Lady are doing a two-part harmony in diminished fifths. I feel like I'm in some kind of shock. I am gripped by a frantic desire to burst into wild fits of laughter.

'Noooo!' Flynn suddenly throws down the guitar, making everyone jump. 'Nina, you were meant to go up a third on that last chord – and then, Dino, you come in with *ta-da-da-da* on the second beat of the last bar! Never mind – now Jennah's here we can have a real soprano for the middle section.'

I get up. 'That was really cool, guys. Thanks for the entertainment.' I smile politely and walk rapidly out of the room.

I head along the corridor looking for the nurses'

station, my heart racing. I hear a door crash open behind me and the sound of running footsteps charging up behind, and I instinctively shrink against the wall to let the person past. But it's Flynn, grabbing me by the shoulders, whirling me round to face him. 'Jen! Jen! You've gotta come back, we need you for the three-part harmony!' He is flushed and sweaty and his eyes are wild.

I struggle to free myself from his grasp. 'Let go of me, Flynn. I mean it. Let go of me! I am *not* going back in there!'

'Stop being silly! Why are you shy? You're a much better singer than any of those others!'

'Flynn, I mean it! I said no!'

'Hey there, what's going on?' A woman is walking briskly down the corridor towards us. 'Flynn, who is this? Aren't you going to introduce us? Why don't you take your hands off her for a minute?'

'Sue, Sue, this is my girlfriend, Jennah, the one I was telling you about.'

Sue flashes me a quick smile and takes hold of Flynn's wrists, pulling his hands firmly away from my shoulders. 'People don't like being grabbed like that, Flynn. Nice to meet you, Jennah. I'm Sue, one of the nurses here. Have you had far to come?'

'London.' My breathing is ragged. I can't believe it has taken a complete stranger to rescue me from my boyfriend. And I can't believe Flynn is behaving like this. Have the doctors here changed his medication?

'Well, the two of you probably want some time to talk. Flynn, why don't you take Jennah down to your room?'

'OK!'

As I move to follow him, Sue points to a thin red cord hanging from the wall. 'Just pull one of these if you need some help,' she says.

I nod, too shocked to reply. Flynn has already disappeared into a room further down. When I come in, he is sitting cross-legged on an unmade bed, jiggling his legs up and down and grinning.

'This is your bedroom?' I say. 'It's pretty decent. I've brought a whole suitcase of your stuff but I left it in the other room. D'you want me to go and get it?'

Flynn pulls himself up to a kneeling position and bounces up and down on the mattress. 'No, stay, stay, stay!' he shouts.

I close the bedroom door and sit down at the end of the bed, my heart still going berserk. 'You're really scaring me, Flynn.'

'I'm just happy to see you! I'm just happy to see you!' he exclaims at the top of his voice.

The mattress continues to rock beneath me. I grab Flynn's arms and attempt to hold him still. 'Shh,' I say. 'Come on, just calm down a bit.'

He continues to bounce. His cheeks are mottled with exertion and there is a demonic look in his eyes. 'What's happened to you?' I ask softly. 'Have they stopped your lithium?'

'No, I'm just full of energy. I'm just full of energy.'

'Please don't say everything twice,' I beg.

'I'm not, I'm not.'

'Yes, you are, Flynn. Surely you can hear it?'

'I can't hear anything. I can't hear anything.'

I close my eyes and take a deep breath. The desire just to get up and walk out is overwhelming.

'Listen to me,' I say slowly. 'You're getting manic again. You need to try and calm yourself down.'

'I will. I will.'

'Try and stop bouncing then.'

'OK, OK.' He suddenly leaps off the bed, almost giving me a heart attack. 'Look what Rami bought me!'

I gaze over in despair. 'Oh, lovely.'

It is a small portable stereo. Flynn kneels down in front of it, adjusting the controls. Tchaikovsky suddenly blares out of the speakers, making me gasp. *Swan Lake.* Oh, great.

'Flynn, could you turn it down? I was really hoping to talk to you a bit.'

He leaps to his feet and strikes a pose, his arms held out. 'Let's dance!'

'Flynn, no!'

Ignoring my protest, he grabs my hands and pulls me off the bed. I start to struggle, then something occurs to me. I can fight this episode of mania and come out the loser, or I can just accept it and let it run its course. I realize that whatever I say or do, I am not going to be able to change his current mood. And at least he is leaping about, wanting to dance, rather than lying semi-conscious in a hospital bed.

Reluctantly I allow myself to be pulled to my feet, and he immediately grabs me and starts twirling me around. The bedroom door swings open, almost knocking us over. It's Sue. 'Fifteen-minute checks,' she says with a smile.

Embarrassed, I try and stop Flynn and his mad waltz around the bedroom.

'Hey, hey, Sue! Look at us dance! Watch, watch!' Flynn grabs me again.

Sue leans against the door frame. 'A musician *and* a dancer,' she says with a grin. 'You're a lucky girl to have him, Jennah.'

'Well, I'm not so sure about the dancer bit,' I gasp as Flynn narrowly misses decapitating me against the wardrobe. He laughs, waltzing me faster and faster, his breath hot against my cheek. I feel my hair flying out behind me. I hold him tightly. Sue is still watching, appearing to enjoy the spectacle. I am so dizzy I have to close my eyes. We collapse on the bed, laughing.

Sue is clapping. 'You two could be contenders for *Strictly Come Dancing*!'

I shake my head with embarrassment and peel myself up from the duvet, panting for breath. Flynn sits on the edge of the bed and holds out his arms to Sue. 'Your turn?'

She shakes her head, laughing. 'I'd tread on your

toes, Flynn. Believe me. I think you're better off sticking with Jennah.'

'Yeah, she's an amazing dancer. And you know what? She's a *fantastic* singer too.'

'Oh, Flynn—' I protest desperately.

'I mean it! When she sings, you feel like you've been touched by an angel.'

'Wow,' Sue says with a smile.

I roll my eyes and shake my head. Flynn doesn't seem to notice. 'I can't even accompany her any more because when she starts to sing, I feel like crying and forget the notes.'

'Flynn, please!' My cheeks are burning and I wonder how much more embarrassed I can get.

Sue flashes me a grin. 'Enjoy it. I wish my other half was so complimentary.'

'Do you know the song *On My Own,* from *Les Misérables*?' Flynn asks her.

'I love that musical,' she replies, her face lighting up.

'Sing it, Jennah!' Flynn commands.

'Flynn, don't be ridiculous—'

'I dunno where my keyboard is, but hold on, I'm sure I could work out the chords pretty easily on the guitar—' He gets up and rushes out of the room.

'I'm so sorry,' I say to Sue. 'And please don't worry, I'm not about to start singing.'

Sue smiles. 'Don't apologize,' she says. 'It's just nice to see him so animated for a change. He was so silent and withdrawn when he first arrived.'

'*Animated* is one way of putting it,' I smile wryly. 'Do you know if they've changed his medication?'

'You'd need to ask the doctor about that,' Sue replies. 'But I believe they're trying him on a new anti-depressant.'

I nod, chewing my lip.

'He talks about you a lot, you know.'

There is a silence. 'Oh . . .'

'He's obviously crazy about you,' Sue said. 'That's something very positive which could help him get better.'

Flynn bounds back into the room, brandishing the guitar.

'I'd better continue my checks,' Sue says with a smile. 'But I'll be listening out for your angelic voice, Jennah.'

Flynn is sitting cross-legged on his pillows, attempting to pick out the dominant chords of the accompaniment to *On My Own*. I get up and make sure the door is firmly closed. 'I'm going to sing it *very* quietly,' I warn him.

To my astonishment, I hear the chords of the accompaniment begin to form. I sigh and smile. 'When on earth did you learn to play the guitar?' I ask. 'This morning?'

Flynn plays me in and looks at me expectantly as my cue approaches. With a nervous glance at the door, I take a breath and begin to sing. Flynn grins at me. His fingers barely hesitate against the strings of the guitar. I watch him as I sing, and I realize he looks different. He looks alive. When I reach the second verse, Flynn joins in, experimenting with some kind of weird harmony. As we sing our rather unique version of *On My Own*, it strikes me that, growing up, this is one thing I never imagined myself doing. Sitting on a bed in a psychiatric hospital with my manic-depressive boyfriend, singing duets on a ropey guitar. But strangely, right now, after everything else that has happened, it doesn't seem so bad.

Chapter Eleven

FLYNN

Her wavy brown hair cascades down her shoulders. Her green eyes shine. Her skin looks like porcelain. I want to kiss her soft mouth. I want to touch her, feel her, taste her. I want to inhale her. Everything about her, from the curve of her collar bone to the way the end of her jeans reveals a strip of bare ankle, seems like absolute perfection. I want to freeze this moment in time and live it for ever. The music, Jennah's voice, Jennah's smile. I feel as if I may burst with happiness. I feel it radiating from my body like an invisible energy force. Her laughing eyes, the dimples in her cheeks, the way the smile lights up her face. Love, that all-powerful, all-consuming life force, rushes through my veins. As we sing, I am flooded with thoughts and feelings. Let the song never end.

Her hand rests against my thigh. I badly need to kiss her. Leaning forwards over the guitar, still playing, my mouth reaches for hers. She laughs, still trying to hum the tune as we kiss. I miss a fret on the guitar. I drop the instrument onto the bed and rise up onto my knees, one hand against her neck, the other in her hair. Jennah stops humming. I kiss her so hard, it hurts. She is the first to come up for breath. 'Flynn—'

I silence her with another kiss, my hand slipping beneath her shirt, moving up the warmth of her stomach. I hardly know where my lips end and hers begin.

'Flynn, wait—'

'Shh.'

Her tongue tastes of peppermint. The curve of her breast is warm against my fingers. Her hair is in my face.

'Flynn – seriously – stop – someone's going to come in—'

'Shh.'

I suck her bottom lip in between my teeth. Press my tongue against hers. Slide my fingers under her bra.

'We can't – don't be silly – we're not allowed – stop it, for goodness' sake!' She is pushing me off, holding me at arm's length.

I sit back on my heels, breathing hard. Jennah is flushed and dishevelled, attempting to straighten her clothes and brush the hair out of her face. I lean forwards and her hand shoots out, pushing me back. 'Don't!' She looks at me, panting a little. 'God, you are unbelievable!' She starts to laugh.

I try to prise her hand off my shoulder. A head appears round the door. 'Fifteen-minute checks,' a voice says.

After the door closes, Jennah whacks me. 'See! I told you!'

'So?' I protest. 'It's not like it's illegal or anything!'

'I should go, it's getting dark,' Jennah says, suddenly sobering. 'I've got a long journey back.'

I feel the smile fade from my face. 'Don't go.'

'I don't want to, but they're going to kick me out soon anyway and I've got a nine o'clock lecture tomorrow.' She smoothes down her hair and gets up from the bed and looks around for her things.

'I'll come back home with you, then.'

'Don't be daft.' She looks afraid suddenly.

I smile to show her that I'm only joking.

The days here are all the same. It is a cross between holiday camp and prison. We are woken by a rap on the door and a cheery voice calling, 'Good morning!' Getting into the bathroom is a feat in itself. While we are having breakfast, they bring us plastic cups with pills. Sometimes there is resistance, and then a long round of bartering ensues. I swallow my 1200 milligrams of lithium carbonate without any fuss. I have learned to pick my battles. Stu is the only one properly awake at breakfast, regaling everyone with a blow-by-blow account of his horrific nightmares. After breakfast I have my appointment with Dr Rasheed, who is encouraging me to work through the feelings leading up to my suicide attempt. I tell her I don't remember much, which is true. After that I return to my bedroom, pick up my laptop and books, then go to the study room, where everyone sits around talking. One of the nurses sits with us, trying to keep the noise down, and on a good day I manage to write part of an essay, or take notes on *Aspects of Wagner*, or work through a couple of chapters for the Aesthetics and Criticism exam. There are various breaks throughout the morning – for cigarettes, meds, coffee – then at twelve thirty we have lunch. After lunch we are allowed to roam around the grounds for a while – which for most of the patients means standing huddled beneath the dripping awning, smoking cigarettes, while I jog along the circumference of the park with Roz, the anorexic beanpole. In the afternoon we do Design and Technology, which is basically another term for art therapy, and I use the Sibelius program that Jennah brought me to do some composition. I am composing a song, a song for Jennah. It is called *Letting Go.*

The afternoon finally comes to an end at four o'clock when we have group therapy. In the evening we have dinner and watch TV, one of the kindlier nurses might honour our request to drive into town for DVDs, and I get in as much practice as I can on my keyboard before they tell me to stop. On Saturday night we go out together as a group – usually to the cinema or to a bowling alley in nearby Brighton. Weekends are freer for most of the inmates – for that is how we see ourselves – Saturdays and Sundays revolving around visitors. Some patients are granted day passes into town for good behaviour and a few long-term ones even get to go home for a night. I get neither, for I am sectioned, and that makes me a prisoner although I haven't even been granted a trial.

Evenings are the worst, because that's when the day begins to feel like it's never going to end and the others on my unit start to really get on my nerves. I get on OK with Stu, who is quite a wit, but when Naz starts banging her head against the wall and Dino starts telling me how he wrote the Bible, it's impossible to forget where I am. Sitting in the claustrophobic room with its tired furniture and flickering TV, the barred windows filled with night, it can be difficult to imagine sinking any lower. I speak to Jennah most evenings, and sometimes it feels like it is only the sound of her voice, the chirpy anecdotes, the thoughts of my life back in London, that keep me alive.

Visits from Rami and my parents are short and strained. I can tell my parents are uncomfortable in the hospital setting, and Rami, presumably feeling guilty about having me sectioned, tries too hard.

They talk about letting me go home at the end of the week, and then it is the next week, and then the week after. I post off my assignments to the Royal College, and Jennah brings me library books at the weekend. I work harder than I ever do at home, just to make time pass faster. I am not allowed to practise for more than three hours a day – they say it is not good for me. I try to explain that five hours a day is what I aspire to at home, but they go on about perfectionist tendencies and obsessive-compulsive behaviour. It makes me laugh – don't they realize that in the world of music, being an obsessive perfectionist is the only way to succeed? But as the days trickle by, the structured regimen, the absence of choices, the suspension of normal life, the daily diet of cognitive behavioural therapy and the increased dose of lithium carbonate combined with a whacking dose of anti-depressants slow me down, dull me, and Dr Rasheed declares that the seesaw of highs and lows is beginning to level out. I leave the psychiatric hospital a whole month after arriving and it is strange: although I have been looking forward to this day the whole time I have been here, I am suddenly afraid.

Rami comes to pick me up and we stop by at the cottage for a civilized lunch with the parents. Mum and Dad seem nervous – about me returning to London, about me going back to the Royal College, about the distant threat of finals . . . I spend most of the meal trying to assure them that I am fully recovered, I am looking forward to going back and everything is going to be fine. I am supposed to be spending the night at my parents', not returning to London till Friday, but I want to surprise Jennah. After a lot of persuasion, I finally get Rami to drive me back home as early dusk begins to gather. We hit rush-hour traffic on the A24 and the journey seems to take for ever. I fiddle with the radio, trying to tune into Classic FM, sidestepping Rami's attempts at brotherly conversation.

Rami drops me off. The flat is unusually tidy, but empty. Christmas Eve seems like a lifetime ago. I find Jennah's new timetable on the notice board and see she has rehearsals this evening. I change into my running shoes, grab my iPod, slam out of the flat and head towards the park. As I enter the gates, I break into a jog. The freezing night air smells of damp earth and wood fires. I cut across the wet grass, taking the quickest route to the other side of the park, relishing the feeling of actually having a destination instead of running round in circles. By the time I reach Kensington High Street, the bottoms of my jeans are soaked and I have a sharp stitch beneath my ribs. I explode through the double-doored entrance of the Royal College into the bright lights of the main hall, flash my pass at the sleepy security guard and then head down towards the sound of raised voices and snippets of music coming from the concert hall.

There is the general mayhem that surrounds any kind of rehearsal, with some members of the orchestra tuning, others chatting, several people wandering around aimlessly, and a harassed-looking Professor Williams talking to Ollie Hendon about voice-box resonance. I walk down the aisle, stopping just short of the clutter of coats and bags and empty music cases, and take a seat in the third row from the front. I spot Harry, deep in conversation with another cellist. Jennah is sitting cross-legged on one of the boxes, looking bored, and it is several minutes before she spots me. When she finally does, her eyes light up and she springs to her feet with a gasp and looks ready to leap off the stage and launch herself into my arms. I motion at her to calm down, but it is too late – Professor Williams has noticed and now he is turning round and peering into the auditorium.

'Flynn!' he exclaims genially. 'To what do we owe this honour?'

I pull an embarrassed face and point to Jennah, reluctant to speak in front of all these people. They know I've been off sick, but they think it's glandular fever. Only Jennah, Harry and Kate know the truth, but even though they have been sworn to secrecy I don't doubt rumours have been going round.

Professor Williams turns back to the orchestra. 'Fabulous!' he exclaims. 'We have a pianist! Which means I can relinquish my position behind the piano and get back to my proper job – which *is*, of course, telling everyone what to do!'

I shrink into my seat. Jennah is laughing. Professor Williams is talking to Ollie Hendon again. I wonder if I can make a run for it.

'OK, OK, quieten down, everyone.' Williams taps his baton against his music stand. The buzz of voices gradually dies. He goes over to the grand piano and holds his arms out towards it, bowing low and looking over at me.

'Oh, for heaven's sake,' I mutter frantically to myself,

burning up with embarrassment. I should never have come. Williams is still standing there in his ridiculous pose, waiting for me. I shake my head vigorously at him. A slow tapping of bows against stands begins in the orchestra. Professor Williams turns and lifts his hands upwards to encourage them. The tapping grows louder. I glare over at Jennah but she raises her hands defensively as if to say, *This has nothing to do with me.* She is grinning though, clearly enjoying herself. I drag myself to my feet. I can feel the blood in my cheeks. Harry lets out a wolf-whistle. I could murder him.

I cross over to the piano. Williams comes up behind me and pats me on the shoulder. 'You didn't think I'd just let you sit there and listen, did you?'

I sit down and adjust the stool and take a look at the music and curse myself for walking into such a trap. Through a fog of noisy chatter, I hear Jennah volunteer herself as my page turner.

'I thought you were my soloist!' Williams protests.

'But I'm on last!'

She gets her way and pulls up a chair beside me as Williams taps his music stand and asks for quiet again. Her eyes are alight. 'I thought you weren't coming back till tomorrow!'

I refuse to look at her, flicking through the music. 'I'm not talking to you right now,' I say. 'This is all your fault.'

'I can't believe you're back!' She begins to laugh.

'Flynn, why are your cheeks so pink?'

'Fuck off.'

She laughs again and puts her hand on my thigh. 'Ooh, I could so kiss you right now.'

'And I could so *hit* you,' I retort.

'Are you two lovebirds ready over there?' Williams calls out. There is laughter from the orchestra. I feel like my face is going to explode.

Jennah's shoulders are still shaking with laughter. 'Oh, Flynn, your face!'

'Shut *up*!' I whisper.

'OK, let's take it from Ollie's song, top of page fifty-nine. Cellos, remember your *adagio*,' Professor Williams instructs.

'It's got three different key signatures,' Jennah informs me.

'I can see that!'

Williams raises his baton and we start ploughing through the Grieg. I struggle to sight-read my way through the piece, not helped by Jennah, who is jiggling with excitement at my side.

'What time did you get back?' she asks me during a break in the piano score.

'Just now. Where's my re-entry?'

'Relax, you've got ages. Did you go back to the flat?'

'Briefly. Do I come in here?'

'No, all this bit is orchestral. Are you pleased to be back?'

'*No.*'

Her shoulders shake with suppressed laughter. 'Liar. You've been talking about this moment for the last two weeks! I can't believe you're finally free of that place!'

'Would have stayed if I'd known I was gonna get roped into this!' I snap. 'How long is this bloody thing going on for?'

'Only till eight. OK, you come back in here. Shit, where are we?' Suddenly panicked, she turns over two pages at once.

'Jennah!'

We grapple with the piano score. Several sheets fall out and flutter softly to the ground. I re-enter with a clash of dissonant chords and Jennah claps a hand to her mouth and snorts with laughter.

I can finally relax when we reach the last piece. I know the accompaniment to *On My Own* so well I don't have to bother with the music. Jennah gets up to sing and I watch her attentively over the top of the piano, careful to place the notes just right, to blend the accompaniment with her voice, to buff it and present it on a pedestal so that it soars above the piano. It is such a pretty, simple song, just her and the piano. The lights from the ceiling catch in her eyes, making them shine. A pretty flush lights up her cheeks. She smiles as she sings, and makes eye-contact with me at every re-entry. She is wearing a faded striped green jumper that is too long in the sleeves, and a long black gypsy skirt that is coming down at the hem. In her ears, I recognize the silver pendants I gave her for Christmas. As the song builds and gathers power, I have to make an effort to concentrate on what I'm supposed to be doing. The piece reaches its crescendo and Jennah's voice hangs in the air, even after I have played the last note. There is a brief silence. Jennah looks over at Professor Williams. He clears his throat. 'Well,' he says. 'Jennah, I think you've found yourself an accompanist for the recital. I don't think even I can compete with that. Would you mind, Flynn? Just for the last piece?'

I nod and shrug as if to say, *What choice do I have?*

Jennah bounces up and down on her toes and claps her hands with glee.

As I am waiting for Jennah to gather up her things, Harry comes over. 'Hey!'

'Hey.'

A pause. Harry looks as if he is desperately trying to formulate some kind of sentence. 'You know – shit – how are you? I've missed you, mate.'

I nod, my eyes suddenly unable to meet his. Suddenly he pulls me into a hug. 'Good to see you back. And in style!' He claps me on the back and turns to Jennah as she approaches. 'Although there seemed to be a bit of confusion during Ollie's song!'

'Jennah was trying to put me off by chucking the piano score around the stage instead of just turning the pages like a normal person,' I inform him, relieved at the sudden change in tone. 'At least she sings better than she turns pages.'

Jennah throws back her head, laughter bubbling out

of her. 'Harry, did you see Flynn's face when Williams asked him to come and play?'

'Yeah, it was like Williams had asked you to come and do a striptease in front of the whole student faculty!' Harry chuckles.

'I don't like sight-reading!' I protest. 'I'm out of practice!'

'You are so easily embarrassed!' Jennah hoots. 'When Williams called us *lovebirds*, I thought you were going to pass out!'

'Very funny,' I grumble.

As Jennah unlocks the door and steps ahead of me into the flat, I circle her waist with my arm, nuzzling her neck. She turns and starts to say something but I silence her with a deep kiss. I pull the long winter coat off her, kicking the door shut behind us, and unwind the multi-coloured scarf from around her neck. Suddenly my hands are in her hair, under her shirt, beneath the waist-band of her skirt. Within seconds we are clawing at each other, shedding items of clothing like leaves from a tree, rolling down onto the carpet, still only half undressed. We are having sex in the narrow hallway, my elbows raw against the rough carpet, and I am alive again.

Chapter Twelve

JENNAH

Having Flynn back, neither manic nor depressed, is wonderful. My soul mate has returned and I'm only just realizing quite how much I have missed him. Not just during his stay at the psychiatric hospital but ever since the bipolar raised its ugly head again back in October. The combination of lithium and anti-depressants he was prescribed during his incarceration, as he likes to call it, seems to be working wonders at keeping both the mania and, more importantly, the dreaded depression at bay. For the first few weeks I am on tenterhooks, watching his every move, every facial expression. Is he talking too much, too rapidly: is he getting manic again? Or is he lethargic, not talking enough: getting depressed again? But he's sticking to his bi-weekly psych appointments, attending bipolar support group meetings, having his blood tested regularly to monitor his lithium levels, keeping in contact with Rami and his parents by phone – and being lovely, lovely towards me. He has written me a song, a song with a simple piano accompaniment, just for me. It is called *Letting Go.* When I first sing it, with Flynn at the piano, it makes me want to cry. It is a sad song – clearly he wasn't feeling too happy when he wrote it – but it is beautiful.

I'd forgotten how romantic he could be, how gentle and sensitive and caring. I'd also forgotten how witty he was. We spend the whole of reading week closeted in the warm fug of the bedsit, oblivious to freezing February mornings and afternoon nightfall, to the thin dusting of snow that paralyses the city. Instead we spend our time cooking languorous meals and drinking cheap red wine, squandering the days on TV and hot baths and sex. We don't even bother answering the phone. Piles of library books lie stacked up against the walls, unopened. When our fridge is empty, we order takeaways. I read Keats, wrapped up in the duvet, Brahms playing softly on the radio. Flynn practises hard for an upcoming competition, the thud of his keyboard audible well into the night.

At the weekend we invite Harry and Kate round for dinner and spend a chilled evening full of red wine and beef casserole, swapping anecdotes from the Royal College, Harry regaling us with tales of his eccentric parents, who want to sell the flat in Bayswater in order to buy themselves a houseboat. At first Kate seems a little on edge around Flynn, but Harry is his usual ebullient self and soon gets her to lighten up. Flynn is animated, his cheeks pink and his eyes bright, and for the first time in ages I think he looks almost happy. I revel in the normality of it all. I begin to relax again. Just sitting around with our friends, chatting and laughing and drinking the night away, feels like an absurd luxury.

On Monday we return to lectures and soon fall back into our usual routine of rushed breakfasts and canteen lunches, rehearsals that spill over into the evening and essays that leak into the night. As winter begins to thaw into spring, I feel a long-needed sense of calm permeate our lives, dotted with student parties and pub-crawls. Harry celebrates his birthday in style. Kate gets accepted onto the music therapy course. Flynn plays for a spot in the finals of the hugely prestigious Queen Charlotte competition.

I sing *Summertime* in a recital at St Martin-in-the-Fields. It is my last public performance before graduation. Mum and Alan come down from Manchester to watch me. Flynn, Harry and Kate join the audience too. My mother and I have reached an uneasy truce regarding my relationship with Flynn. I know she is still deeply worried but after I told her she was just making things worse for me, she reluctantly agreed to leave the subject alone – for the time being at least. When I come off the stage to the sound of healthy applause, I feel suddenly sad, almost tearful. My last performance with the Royal College. My four years as a music student in London are coming to a close. The end of an era. At the after-concert party, my tutor introduces me to a Madame Françoise Denier – a well-known opera singer from my mother's generation. She asks me what my plans are for when I graduate. I tell her that I haven't given it much thought, which isn't strictly true. But knowing that Flynn is going to be on the road for most of next year has made me nervous. I like the idea of teaching, but am reluctant to tie myself down to a full-time job.

Françoise Denier is telling me about the Paris Conservatoire where she teaches. After a few minutes I suddenly realize where she is going with this conversation. And then she comes out with it: would I be interested in doing a one-year graduate course at the Conservatoire de Paris under her tutelage? She is confident that I would get a full scholarship, and my voice apparently has a clarity and resonance that she finds unique. I am absurdly flattered and even feel a brief flutter of excitement, but I smile politely and say that moving to Paris for a year is out of the question. I am relieved she doesn't ask why. I don't want her to know that I plan to become a freelance flute teacher so that I can travel with Flynn to his concerts whenever possible. I don't want to have to explain how much I am willing to sacrifice, how much I love him. But before she moves off, she hands me her business card and tells me to call her if I ever change my mind.

Yet as the weeks roll by and I begin to believe that the doctors have finally found the perfect drug combination to keep Flynn well for the rest of his life, a slither of thought, an unwanted intrusion, pricks at the back of my mind. I don't want to let it in, don't even want to be forced to acknowledge it, but it's there nonetheless, a shadowy backdrop to an idyllic end of term. It appears to me in my dreams as a door right before me, a door I know I must open, but I am terrified – terrified of what lies in wait. I know that if the dreams are to stop, if the nagging in my brain is to cease, I must face my fears and open that door, but I can't, I can't. I just *can't.* Then, one morning, I am hurled against it; the door is forced open against my will. One morning I wake up and the sun is high in the sky and Flynn is still asleep, his arm draped over my chest.

He wakes with a start at my shout and grabs me by the wrist. 'What? What?'

I am having a panic attack. I've never had one before but I know that's what this is, because I suddenly feel as if I can't get enough air into my lungs and so I cup my hands over my nose and mouth and try to take in less oxygen. I scrunch up against the head of the bed and try to elbow Flynn away. He looks faintly comical – his hair on end, the imprint of the pillow still fresh on his cheek, his blue eyes wide with fright – and I begin to calm down.

'I'm OK.' I lower my hands tentatively from my face and attempt to breathe normally, trying to focus on a lopsided picture on the wall of the two of us on holiday.

'Were you having a nightmare?' Flynn is kneeling up on the bed, looking down at me with concern, his once-white T-shirt hanging over his green checked boxer shorts. I focus on the details, just the details. If I stay in the present, everything will be all right. But I am shaky, I've come too close, the door is already open and I have to step through.

I look at him. 'There's something I've been wanting to ask you. Ever since – ever since Boxing Day.' I can feel my heart.

He drops his hand from my wrist and sits back on his heels. When his eyes meet mine, they are wary, almost afraid. The look on his face nearly forces me back, but I keep going forward.

'I'm sorry,' I say. 'I know you don't want to be reminded of that time and I don't either. But I think I have to talk about it. Just this once. Or I feel like I'll never be able to put it completely behind me.'

He hasn't moved from his kneeling position, his arms loose by his sides. He is gnawing at his lower lip; I know what that means and I want to retreat, retract.

'I need to know why.'

'I wasn't well, Jennah.' The colour has risen to his cheeks and his discomfort is palpable. It almost feels like shame.

'I know, my love, I know. And I'm not angry. Not any more. But I just want to know – did you think – when you took all those pills and got into bed beside me – did you think of what it would be like for me, when I woke up, if – if you hadn't still been breathing? If – if it had worked as you'd wanted it to? If you had died?' My voice is shaky, the words catch in my throat, but I've done it, I've asked the question I'd dreaded asking.

He looks down at his knees, the colour still high in his cheeks, and I can see the rapid rise and fall of his chest beneath his T-shirt. I want to reach out, touch him, say that it's OK, but I can't.

'No.' He says in barely a whisper. He does not look up.

'Why?' The word quivers infuriatingly.

I'm not even sure he is going to reply. I count his breaths. Seven, eight, nine . . .

'Because – because when you feel that bad, that low, you stop caring. About everything and everyone. You can only think of yourself.' His voice is hoarse, hesitant and barely audible, as if he is having to force the words out. 'The pain is so . . . big, it takes up all the space in your body, in your mind, and there isn't room for anything else. All you can think about is your own suffering, and how to stop it – you'd do anything to stop it. Anything. I really mean anything.' He looks at me now as if imploring me to understand, chewing savagely on the corner of his lip, and I realize with a shock that he is close to tears.

'What does it feel like?'

He shakes his head and looks away from me, out of the window at the bright late-morning sun. 'You don't want to know—'

'God, Flynn. I love you.' My voice cracks. 'Of course I do.' I swallow hard, trying to suppress the rising ball of pain at the back of my throat.

'I can't explain it . . .'

'Try.'

'It's just this pain, this unbearable mental pain – often it's your body too, and every part of you hurts. But you don't really care about your body, it's your mind. Every thought hurts like hell. Everything you see is awful, twisted, pointless. And the worst – the worst of it is yourself. You realize you are the most ghastly person in the world, the most hideous, inside and out. And you just want to escape, you just want to get rid of yourself, of your suffering, of the pain inside your head. You want to shut out the world and yourself, for ever. A-and death is the only option left because you've been through this time and time again, thought and thought about trying to change yourself, the way you think, the way you behave, the way you live. Yet it always comes back to this – the fact that you just d-don't want to be alive—' He breaks off, turning away suddenly, pressing his fingers to his eyes.

I stare at the back of his head. My eyes sting, my throat aches. I *want* to hear this, I *want* to understand, but at the same time it hurts, on so many different levels. It hurts to hear that he can reach a place where he doesn't care about me any more, doesn't care about damaging me so much I might never recover. It also hurts to hear him say it, to hear him verbalize even in the most simplistic terms the agony he was going through, has been through time and time again, while I remained blissfully unaware.

I move towards him on the bed and try to touch him but he holds out his hand to keep me at bay.

'Flynn . . .'

'I-I'm OK!'

'I know you're OK. I just want to touch you.'

He pulls away almost angrily and goes to the window, resting his forehead against the glass, his arms crossed above his head.

I clench my teeth together, wincing against the tidal wave of sobs that threaten to engulf me.

'I'm sorry, Flynn, I just needed to try and understand. I didn't mean to bring it all back.' The bedsprings creak as I get up. Suddenly I am afraid.

'Don't go!' He shouts the words, making me start, whirling round to face me, his flushed face awash with tears.

'I'm not going anywhere!' I exclaim. 'I'm just frightened – I'm so frightened it's going to happen again!' I step into his arms and burst into tears.

'No, Jennah, don't – don't . . .' His face is hot and wet against mine and he holds me tight, stroking the back of my head.

'Did you think I – I would be able to carry on, without you?' I sob, my voice muffled against his shoulder. 'Did you think I'd manage to get through this thing called life without you by my side?'

'I thought you'd be better off without me – I didn't think, I couldn't think . . .' We are both sobbing now.

'Who else would run out on their own birthday party,

force me barefoot down the fire escape, bring me fruit salad in bed, complain that I'm humming a pop song in the wrong key?' I am laughing and crying at once. 'Who else would force me to dance in front of a complete stranger, learn to play the guitar overnight and accompany me when I sing?' I sniff hard and punch him on the shoulder. 'How could I possibly live without you, you stupid, stupid idiot?'

Flynn steps back and grabs a pillow off the bed. 'Fine, if you're going to get physical about it—'

I lunge for the other pillow but he hits me squarely on the top of the head. 'Well, you've done it now – you can never complain about any of my harebrained schemes ever again— *Ow!* Jennah, why can't you just fight like a girl? Why do you always have to be so bloody vicious?'

One of the pillows finally splits and we collapse, exhausted, on the floor, surrounded by white feathers. I rest my head on Flynn's chest and listen to the pounding of his heart. He stares up at the ceiling, wiping the sweat from his brow. 'What's the betting you can't go for one hour without getting out the vacuum cleaner?'

'What are you talking about? I'm not some kind of neatness freak!'

His chest vibrates with laughter. 'OK. Bet you five pounds.'

'Why not make it ten?' I retort.

'Fine. Ten pounds it is.'

I raise my wrist to look at my watch.

Flynn laughs again. 'An hour is a long time, Jennah. I wouldn't start counting down the minutes quite yet.'

I turn my head on his chest in order to give him a nasty smile. 'I was checking to see what time I would be collecting my money.'

'Oh, and there's another condition,' Flynn adds. 'We have to lie in this mess until the hour is up.'

I jack-knife up. 'That's not fair! We can't sit here the whole time. What are we going to do, stuck in the bedroom for a whole hour?'

Flynn gives me a mischievous grin and pulls me back down on top of him. 'I can think of a whole bunch of things, Jennah.'

'Well, if you're going to get creative . . . Wait—' I hold him off, sobering for a moment. 'Promise me one thing?' I stare into his clear blue eyes, just centimetres away from mine. 'Next time, when you feel that bad, when you feel even slightly depressed – will you tell me? Even if you're convinced it won't make a difference, or even if you think it might make things worse, will you just promise – promise to let me know?'

'I promise,' he says, and then bites my nose.

The day before the Easter weekend, Flynn receives a phone call. It's from Professor Kaiser. Flynn has made it to the finals of the Queen Charlotte competition. He slams down the phone, bounds onto the sofa and whoops with joy. The Queen Charlotte International

Music Competition. Held every four years in Brussels, it attracts top musicians from all over the world. It is one of the Big Four, one that Flynn really wants to win. He whirls me round and round till my head is spinning and I beg for him to stop. I am effervescent with joy. After everything – everything he has been through, he deserved something like this. He deserved it so much. But I am also in awe. A psychotic episode, months of depression, a breakdown at Christmas, a month incarcerated in a psychiatric hospital, and still he manages to pull this off. Years ago at music camp Harry once said to me, 'He's not just a musical prodigy, you know. He's a musical *genius*.' It comes back to me now. And I laugh when I kiss my 'musical genius' because really he's just Flynn.

After Easter Rami and Sophie invite us over for lunch. Aurora is walking now even though she hasn't yet reached her first birthday. We sit around in the spacious living room. Rami is glued to the television as his favourite team battle against relegation. Aurora takes my hand and I allow her to lead me over to her toy box on the far side of the room. Sophie smiles over at us from the sofa. 'Oh, we are so happy to have a change from Mummy,' she says as Aurora coos and claps her hands with pleasure.

'I think she remembers me,' I say to Sophie. 'She gave me such a big smile when we arrived.'

'Of course she remembers you!' Sophie exclaims. 'She absolutely adores her auntie Jennah.'

I feel myself flush with pleasure. I have never been called an auntie before. I plant a big kiss on the top of Aurora's head. Flynn enters with a tray of coffees. He hands them round and then comes over to us, waving a biscuit in front of Aurora. 'Can she?' he suddenly remembers to ask Sophie.

'Of course, if Jennah doesn't mind biscuit crumbs all over her.'

Flynn gives Aurora the biscuit. I pretend to try and bite a piece of it and Aurora generously sticks the salivary biscuit straight into my open mouth. We all laugh.

Flynn goes back to his coffee and takes a seat on the sofa next to Sophie.

I pretend I'm a monster, trying to bite Aurora's toe. She wiggles and squeals.

Out of the corner of my eye, I notice Sophie putting her arm around Flynn's shoulders, pulling him towards her and kissing the side of his face. 'How's my favourite brother-in-law?'

He flushes briefly and smiles. 'Your *only* brother-in-law.'

I nibble on Aurora's toe. She squeals, banging her feet against the floor.

'Still my favourite,' Sophie says, ruffling his hair affectionately. 'Are you feeling as well as you look?'

'I think so,' Flynn replies.

Aurora starts to chortle as I blow raspberries into her tummy.

'That's fabulous,' Sophie says. 'What about your hands?'

'They're still the same, unfortunately,' Flynn replies, suddenly lowering his voice.

'So the Lithobid's not working?'

'No.'

I stop, my face buried in Aurora's lap.

'Show me – is it visible?' Sophie asks.

I withdraw my head from Aurora's clutches, glancing surreptitiously across the room. Flynn has his hands held out in front of him, splaying his long fingers with their bitten-down nails. Sophie seems to be inspecting them.

'I can see what you mean,' I hear her say. 'What was Doctor Stefan's reaction?'

'That I have to live with it, basically. He won't lower the lithium until I've been well for at least six months.' Flynn is talking so quietly now that I have to strain to hear. 'I tried asking him about switching to Sodium Valproate or Carbamazepine but since they weren't very effective when I first tried them he says he doesn't want to risk it.'

Aurora tugs at my hair and babbles loudly, trying to engage me in further play. I blow into her tummy again so that they won't think I'm listening.

'Is it difficult to live with?' Sophie asks.

'It really affects my playing,' Flynn replies.

Aurora starts to wail in protest at my inertia. I force myself to pay attention to her and try building her a tower of Duplo. She smiles and gurgles at me, happy again. I try to keep her as quiet as I can, straining to catch the conversation on the other side of the room, over the noise of Rami's football match.

'I suppose you could ask Doctor Stefan for a med called Propranolol, but it can cause sleep disturbances.'

'I'll try anything,' Flynn says. 'I've got to stop this, Soph – it could ruin my career.'

'I know, but you're well. Look at you, you're so well.'

'But none of that matters if I can't play.'

On the train home, I sit with my legs crossed at the ankles, feet up on the seat in front, head resting against Flynn's chest. He has his arms around me and I feel strangely safe in the empty, chilly carriage. He is practising the fingering to the Rach Two on my thighs. I recognize it from the opening volley of chords. I turn my head slightly to look up at his face and say, 'How many more days till the Queen Charlotte finals?'

'Twenty-three,' he replies without missing a beat.

Harry, Kate and I have all booked tickets on the Eurostar to watch him compete. Harry's parents live in Brussels, so we don't even have to pay for a hotel.

'What were you saying to Sophie about your hands?' I ask suddenly.

I feel Flynn stiffen. There is a silence. 'Nothing much. Just that the higher dose of lithium was giving me a slight hand tremor. But it's fine now. It's wearing off.'

'Really?' I turn to look at him again. 'Isn't it affecting your playing?'

'No, no, not any more. It's hardly noticeable. Just a minor nuisance from time to time.'

For the next few weeks we don't see much of each other. University continues at its frenetic pace and Flynn takes time out from all his lectures to practise for the competition. Finals are just over a month away and my revision begins in earnest. The weekend trip to Brussels draws nearer, a welcome break from the long hours spent in the library. Harry calls the night before with confirmation of train times and meeting points. Professor Kaiser calls to give Flynn some last-minute reminders. The professor is catching a train on the day of the competition, so thankfully he won't be travelling with us. That night, I manage to persuade Flynn to stop practising by ten. I go to bed with the sickish feeling I get whenever I am about to watch him compete.

The following morning I wake up in an empty bed to the sound of my alarm clock. After showering, dressing and doing some last-minute packing, I find Flynn at his keyboard, headphones clamped over his ears.

'How long have you been up?' I ask him, pulling off the headphones.

He doesn't turn round. 'An hour or so. Oh, good, now you're awake I can use the piano.'

I look at him suspiciously as he crosses over to the upright, pulling his stool with him. I wonder if he has slept at all. His eyes have that bright, shiny look he always gets before a major competition. I go into the kitchen to make coffee and toast. I manage to drag Flynn away from the piano long enough to down some coffee, but can't get him to touch the toast. He looks excited and on edge, jiggling his knees up and down, making the whole table vibrate.

'We need to go,' he says.

I take another bite of my toast. I am definitely not awake yet. 'The train's not till ten.'

'We're meeting Harry and Kate at nine.'

'I know, but it won't take us more than an hour to get to St Pancreas,' I point out reasonably.

'What if there are delays?'

'Flynn, it's quarter past seven!'

'Yeah, I know. We should go.'

I give him a steady look. 'We'll go in ten minutes. Let me finish my breakfast in peace.'

He fixes me with an urgent stare. The colour is high in his cheeks. 'Maybe there'll be a bomb scare . . .'

'Are you trying to give me indigestion?'

'I just really think we should go.'

'Fine.' I give in with a sigh, drain my cup, get up and put the plates in the sink. Flynn jumps up and bounds out of the room, returning seconds later with our rucksacks.

'We're going to be *so* early,' I complain in the hallway, pulling on my jacket. 'We'll probably get there in half an hour and then we'll have a whole hour to kill until the others arrive.'

He ignores me, opening the front door.

'Wait,' I say. 'At the risk of sounding like your mother, have you got everything? Music? Meds?'

'Yes,' he calls back, already galloping down the stairs.

I lock the door behind me and follow him down. As we emerge into the street, a thought occurs to me. 'Hold on. I've forgotten something . . .'

Flynn rolls his eyes in exasperation and starts striding off down the street. 'Catch me up at the station!' he shouts back over his shoulder.

Biting back a wave of irritation, I remind myself that Flynn is always a nightmare before a big competition and hurry back upstairs to the flat. Leaving my keys in the door, I run down the hall to the bathroom. I know I'm being an incorrigible mother hen, but it has just occurred to me that it would be no bad idea to take a second supply of meds. If Flynn were to lose his bag, which seems infinitely possible in his current mood, at least we wouldn't be up shit creek.

I squat down in front of the medicine cabinet and yank open the bottom drawer. I start to reach inside, and then I freeze. A faint ringing sound begins in my ears. The drawer is packed full of medicine boxes. Boxes and boxes, crammed one on top of the other. With considerable difficulty, I start pulling them out, my hands beginning to shake. LITHIUM CARBONATE, LITHIUM CARBONATE, LITHIUM CARBONATE. I open the first few boxes. All full, packed tight with untouched blister packs, the cardboard sides bulging. I check the sticky labels. Flynn's name in capital letters. The new dose, 1200 milligrams daily. And at the top right-hand corner, the prescription date: 4 April, 4 April, 4 April, 2 May, 2 May . . . I can feel myself start to shake. 'No, no, no,' I am whispering to myself. I start pulling the boxes open. They are all completely full. Not a single tablet has been removed from its blister pack. A cold panic descends over me. A hundred different scenarios race through my mind. Do I call the professor and tell him Flynn can't compete? Do I call Harry's mobile and tell him the trip is off? Do I wait here for Flynn to come back and find me? Or do I run to the tube station to confront him? Have a screaming match in the middle of the street? All options are equally horrendous.

Finally, with fumbling hands, I start shoving the blister packs back into the boxes, and the boxes back into the drawer. I keep one blister pack and put it in my coat pocket just in case, although since it's clear Flynn stopped taking his lithium two months ago, there seems little point.

Waiting for me in the mouth of the tube station, Flynn is beside himself. 'What took you so long? We're going to be late!'

I bite my lip to stop myself from snapping in reply and follow him down the escalators to the platform. In the packed carriage, I can still feel my heart racing. The options continue to rush through my mind. Can I call it off? *Should* I call it off? No. Flynn will just go on to

Brussels without me. And I risk seriously messing up his chances in the competition if I make a scene now. There is actually nothing I can do. Nothing until after the competition. And even then . . . There are two months' worth of lithium tablets in that drawer. So he decided to stop taking his lithium after that lunch at Rami and Sophie's. It is obviously a calculated decision. It is obviously a long-term one. How do I stand any chance of changing his mind? I look across the crowded carriage at him – the wide blue eyes, the pink flush of excitement in his cheeks, the tousled blond hair – he looks so alive. Without meaning to, I find myself thinking back to the waxy, inert figure hooked up to tubes in the hospital bed. I clench my teeth together to repress the urge to scream.

When Harry hugs me hello, I want to hold onto him. As I draw away, he looks at me and says, 'Hey, cheer up, you're not the one that's meant to be strung-out!' I force a painful smile. Harry and Kate are all chatty and excited, Flynn is charging on ahead through the automated ticket machines. We sit around in the departure lounge for what seems like hours, Flynn pacing the floor and Kate chatting to me about her revision timetable, until finally we are able to board the train. In the quiet air-conditioned carriage, we sit facing each other across a small table. Around us, the seats quickly fill with passengers. Flynn, wedged between me and the window, plugs into his iPod, closes his eyes and practises the fingering to the concerto against the edge of the table.

Harry flashes me a sympathetic grin. 'At least after this one you'll get a break from the Rach Two, won't you?'

'For a bit,' I reply. 'But then there's the Leeds International at the end of August. So that'll be fun.' I flash him a wry smile.

Harry laughs. 'Oh, Jen, you sound like the concert-weary wife.'

We arrive in Brussels in the early afternoon. Harry's mother, Diane, is at the station to pick us up. She is a petite, well-dressed woman, as unlike Harry as you could imagine. In the car, Flynn sits in the front, chatting away to Diane. I hear my name mentioned several times.

'Are you all right, Jen?' Harry looks at me suddenly.

'Yes,' I say quickly.

'What do you girls think of Brussels, then?' Harry asks with a grin, peering out at the grey, rain-soaked city. Kate laughs in reply and I force a smile.

Harry's parents live in a spacious house just outside the city centre. Flynn and I are given one guest room, Harry and Kate the other. Paul, Harry's father, is an older version of Harry, laid-back and jovial. He has aged since I saw him last. Dinner is a three-course meal with napkins and a tablecloth. The talk revolves around the Royal College, finals, Flynn's competition. At one point Diane brings in a large framed photograph of Harry, Flynn and me when we were at music camp together. We are sitting atop a huge fallen log in the camp's grounds.

Kate bursts out laughing. 'God, look at you three, you were all so cute! How old were you then?'

'It was the year we all first met,' Harry replies, grinning. 'We must have been ten or eleven.'

'Flynn looks so sweet,' Kate says. 'Like a little angel.'

Flynn narrows his eyes at her in mock annoyance.

'Oh, but he wasn't,' Diane says, giving Flynn an affectionate smile. 'He was like one of those Duracell bunnies, constantly on the go. Used to drive poor Maria spare.'

'Look at Jennah,' Paul says, pointing to the messy-haired girl in dirty jeans with the dimple-cheeked grin. 'Smiling away as if butter wouldn't melt in her mouth. Oh, she was such a tomboy. Always in trouble. Worse than the boys!'

'Hey!' I protest, feeling myself blush.

'Yeah, yeah, she was,' Flynn chips in. 'And she was always so bossy, always deciding where we'd go, what games we'd play. She still is, you know. Some things never change.'

I turn to him in mock outrage. 'I'm not bossy!'

He starts to laugh. 'Yeah, right. You're worse than my mother! It's like, *Pick your clothes up off the floor, Flynn; You're practising too much, Flynn; Peel the potatoes before you mash them, Flynn; It's your turn to do the washing-up, Flynn . . .*'

Everyone laughs.

I roll my eyes, the heat rising to my face. 'He's exaggerating, as usual.'

'I swear it's worse than being back at home,' Flynn goes on, clearly enjoying himself. 'It's enough to drive anyone crazy. Nag, nag, nag, all day long—'

'Oh, come on.' Harry comes to my rescue. 'Jennah's hardly a nag—'

'And she's so fussy!' Flynn continues. 'Talk about OCD. Everything has to go in its right place: pencils parallel to the edge of the desk, books flush with the edge of the shelves—'

'I never do that!' I exclaim in astonishment.

'She even irons her own knickers!' Flynn exclaims in a flourish.

'That's a complete lie!'

Kate, Diane and Paul are laughing. Only Harry seems aware of my plight. He puts a restraining hand on Flynn's arm. 'Hey, ease up. I think that's a bit of an exaggeration . . .'

'Gag him, Harry,' I implore, tears of frustration suddenly springing to my eyes.

Kate, still laughing, notices my face. 'Hey, hey, stop,' she says to Flynn. 'Poor Jennah. Come on, just because she's tidy and you're not—'

'And you couldn't even imagine what she's like in bed—'

'Stop it!' I half rise from my seat, my cheeks burning. I don't know if I'm trying not to laugh, or trying not to cry. 'Stop it right now!'

'She's like, *Right, you lie there and—*'

'Flynn!' I shout furiously.

'And I'm going to . . .'

I walk out. I am down the corridor and out of the front door and halfway down the darkened, rain-soaked street before I fully realize what I am doing. Even then I am only aware that I can't walk fast enough and that my knees feel weak. Hugging myself against the cold, I hurry down one street and then another, not knowing where I am going, only wanting to put as much distance between myself and the dinner table as possible. As I walk, a slow painful thought begins to penetrate the fog inside my brain. *Jennah, it's rude to walk out on someone else's dinner. It's shamefully, shockingly rude.*

I take in great lungfuls of cold night air, trying desperately to fight back the tears. I can barely believe it. I can barely believe that Flynn, my boyfriend, the person I love most in the whole world, would do that. I see the bright gleam in his eyes, the laughter at my rising discomfort, the revelling in my excruciating embarrassment. Couldn't he see that he was going too far? Couldn't he see that he was being cruel? Harry had, Kate had, even Harry's parents were looking uncomfortable towards the end. But he just went blithely on, loving it, not caring that I was dying with humiliation.

A voice breaks the silence behind me. I walk faster but there are running feet on the pavement behind me, someone touching my arm. Flynn, come to apologize? Flynn, come to say he is so sorry, he didn't know what he was thinking?

'Jennah, hey, slow down. Put this on, for goodness' sake.' Harry. He wraps his jacket around me.

'Harry, I'm sorry, I'm so sorry about your parents—' I start to cry.

He pulls me into a hug. 'Hey, don't worry about my parents. You're like a daughter to them. They understand. Jesus, you're shaking.' He tightens his arms around me. 'Oh, Jen, Flynn's being an idiot, a completely insensitive idiot, but I'm sure he didn't mean to upset you that much—'

'He doesn't care!' I sob against Harry's chest. 'He saw how embarrassed I was getting! It just amused him! It j-just spurred him on! A-and talking about sex in front of your *parents*!'

'I know. He doesn't seem himself. Maybe he's stressed about the competition and this is his way of dealing with it. He's been acting pretty weird all day.'

'He's g-getting manic again!' I sob.

'No, no. I'm sure it's just the stress of the concert . . .' Harry tries to reassure me.

'It's not that! He *is* getting m-manic again! He's stopped taking his lithium!'

There is a silence. I hear Harry inhale sharply. Then he starts to walk, taking me by the hand. 'Come on, let's go to a café and sit down.' He reaches down into the pocket of the jacket I am now wearing and retrieves his mobile. I hear him speak to Kate, tell her he is taking me to a quiet place to calm down. I hear him assure her I'm going to be fine. I wish I could be so sure.

In the gentle warmth of the near-empty café, Harry and I face each other over two cups of steaming coffee. I use the napkin to wipe my face as best I can, scraping my hair back, trying to shed the role of hysterical-crying-female. Harry's face is pinched and grave.

'Are you sure?' he asks me.

I nod and sniff, fighting back a fresh wave of tears. 'I found all the boxes this morning. There were a whole two months worth, all crammed into the drawer.'

'And you haven't confronted him?'

'I didn't want to mess up his chances in the competition!'

There is a silence. Then Harry sighs. 'Yeah, I can understand that.' He is frowning down at the tabletop, his brows knitted together in thought. 'Oh fuck,' he breathes.

I bite my lip, inhaling deeply. Harry looks up at me. 'Any idea why?'

I tell him about the conversation I overheard about the tremor in Flynn's hands.

'That would make sense,' Harry responds. 'I remember him complaining about his hands shaking when he first started taking the drug.'

'But then it wore off,' I protest. 'I'm sure it would have this time if only he'd given his body a chance to get used to the higher dose.'

'He's still taking his anti-depressants though, right?'

'I – I think so. I didn't see any of them lying around.'

'Then he probably is,' Harry tries to reassure me.

'Which is something. It will hopefully keep him from dropping down as low as he did at Christmas. The problem now is how to stop him from getting too manic.'

'I've got one of the packets of lithium with me,' I tell him. 'Maybe we could crush a pill and put it in his coffee or something . . .' I am grasping at straws.

'It wouldn't work long-term. And he'd guess what you'd done as soon as the side-effects came back,' Harry replies sensibly. 'I think the only thing you can do is talk to him about it. Tell him you know. Tell him how upset and frightened it's making you feel. Try and persuade him—'

'Tonight?' I look at Harry, softly aghast.

'No, no, you're right. You can't do anything until after the concert,' Harry says. 'And even if you did manage to talk him into taking a pill tonight, it wouldn't do him much good for tomorrow. Apparently that stuff takes weeks to kick in.'

We finish our coffee in silence. We walk back to the house, Harry's arm linked with mine. I am no longer crying and I do feel slightly better. But I wish there was some way of avoiding Flynn.

I apologize to Diane about three times that evening. Finally she gives me a hug and says if I apologize again, she is going to throttle me. I meet Kate on the stairs outside the bathroom and she asks if I'm all right. I nod and force a smile.

I take a very long time in the bathroom, thawing gently under the steaming shower, hoping against hope that when I return to the guest bedroom, Flynn will have dropped off to sleep. But he is sitting fully-dressed against the headboard, doing finger exercises against his thighs. I go over to the mirror and start brushing out the wet tangles in my hair.

'Where did you take off to so suddenly?' he asks me casually.

I take a deep breath and don't turn round. 'I wasn't feeling very well. I just needed some air.'

He says nothing. I glance at him in the mirror and see that he's gone back to doing his finger exercises. He doesn't seem in the slightest bit perturbed by my lame excuse. I bite my lip, hard, and concentrate on my hair. 'We should get an early night,' I say. 'Because of tomorrow.' It is not yet ten o'clock but I just want to turn off the light and crawl into bed.

'Yeah, OK.' Flynn has his sheet music spread out over the duvet. He doesn't even look up.

I finish with my hair, glance at my puffy eyes in the mirror and decide I have had enough of this day. I climb into one side of the bed and pull the covers up to my chin. 'Goodnight,' I say.

'Are you going to sleep right this second?' Flynn asks, sounding surprised.

I decide it's better if I don't answer. Perhaps, if I try hard enough, I can will myself asleep even with the overhead light on.

After a few minutes there is the sound of shuffling papers, creaky floorboards and the zip of his rucksack opening and closing. I can hear Flynn kicking off his jeans, not bothering to pick them up off the floor. I feel his weight descend onto the mattress. I hug the duvet tighter around me. He rolls over. Suddenly his arms are around my waist, pulling me backwards towards him. 'No,' I protest, pulling away. 'I'm sleepy.'

'You're not sleepy.' Flynn's breath is hot against my neck. His arms tighten around me. 'You so turn me on when you play hard to get.'

I half turn my head. 'I'm not playing hard to get,' I say coldly. 'I'm really tired and I'm not in the mood. Goodnight.'

I press my cheek back to the pillow. Flynn's hands slide up beneath my T-shirt.

I shove him hard. 'Get off me!' I surprise myself with the force of my own shout.

There is a silence. I roll over onto my back. Flynn is propped up on one elbow, looking down at me, his face registering hurt and bewilderment. I reach out and switch off the light.

The following afternoon Harry, Kate and I do some sightseeing while Flynn is in rehearsals at the concert hall. After trailing round the small city for a few hours, we reconvene in a café and spend the rest of the afternoon sipping lattes and eating waffles. At half past six we make our way back to the Palais des Beaux-Arts, a vast, grey, stone-pillared monument lined with flags. We feel distinctly under-dressed and bedraggled from the persistent drizzle as we follow the elegantly turned-out French and Flemish speakers into the large auditorium. Normally this would be the moment when my heart starts to pound, when I feel myself oscillating between pleasure and pain. But today I feel only a dull ache, a hollowness. Harry and Kate make up for it though, keeping me entertained with nervous, excited chatter and poring over the order of play, counting Flynn's place in the running order. I try to join in, but my cheek muscles ache from the effort of smiling. I am relieved when the lights go down and a hush descends.

The first few competitors are good, really good. As usual the standard is impossibly high and, not for the first time, I am relieved I decided against pursuing performing as a full-time career. All this competing, all this trying to make a name for yourself. You have to be good, so good, not just a workaholic but also obscenely talented. And the higher you go, the greater the investment of time, money and energy, the steeper the fall . . . It's at times like these that Kate can feel relieved about her music therapy course, that Harry can feel comforted by the thought of a career in music technology, that I can feel thankful that I love teaching and music teachers are in demand. We listen to a dazzling Beethoven concerto, followed by a staggering Brahms concerto, followed by a magnificent Grieg concerto.

Then Kate's elbow digs painfully into my side and we all three hold our breath.

Flynn comes on, as always looking completely alien to me in his black suit and blue tie. Only the shock of fair hair bears any similarity to the scruffy boyfriend who kissed me goodbye that morning. I notice Professor Kaiser's back stiffen, two rows in front. Flynn sits, spends an eternity adjusting the stool, touches the pedal and the keys. As usual when he performs, he looks scarily serious, his blue eyes fierce. The conductor turns. Flynn looks up at him, presses his lips together, then nods. The conductor turns back to face the orchestra. The silence is overpowering.

As soon as the dramatic introduction to Rachmaninov's Second Piano Concerto begins, I know I am going to cry. I bite my tongue even though the lights are dim because I figure I cry far too much over Flynn as it is. It's not the piece – I've heard it millions of times before – but something about seeing him in front of an audience, vulnerable, exposed. I know how much practice has gone into this concerto, just for this one moment. I know how much he wants to win. It's not that the other competitors don't deserve to win too, it's just that Flynn, with all he has to cope with, somehow seems to deserve it more. I try to concentrate on being objective, try comparing his performance to the three who have gone before him, but it's hard. There is something singular, distinctive, indefinable about his playing that allows me to recognize him even with my eyes closed. I find myself holding my breath as he goes through the series of impossibly difficult cadential harmonies that I know he was having difficulty with in his last lesson. I stare at his profile, the eyes narrowed in concentration, the colour high in his cheeks, and I think, *I love you, I love you so much.* Kate glances at me and takes my hand, squeezing it tight as Flynn races through a dramatic volley of chords. The second movement is exquisite. He makes the piano sing. The final movement is dark and dramatic: he plays with an explosive anger that is almost frightening. The final sequence of arpeggios practically sweeps him off the piano stool. The audience erupts.

He shakes hands with the conductor, bows briefly and then exits the stage hurriedly, as if late for another appointment. We have to sit through another three concertos before the interval, during which the judges cast their votes. I make polite conversation with Professor Kaiser in the foyer while Harry and Kate play 'spot the music parent'. When we are called back to the auditorium, my knees suddenly feel weak.

After a speech, the prizewinners are announced. Third prize goes to a Japanese girl. Second prize makes me hold my breath. It isn't Flynn. First prize . . . As usual there is a dramatic pause. I feel as if my heart is going to burst . . .

'Flynn Laukonen.'

Harry and Kate leap to their feet. The audience bursts into applause. Harry and Kate are jumping up and down.

I haven't moved. Harry is grabbing me by the shoulders, shaking me brutally. 'He won, he won, he won!'

The people sitting around us turn in their seats to look at us with a smile. Flynn comes onto the stage to accept his award. It is a giant steel treble clef – not very original. But he also gets a cheque for 12,000 euros. That will come in useful for paying the rent next year. He looks embarrassed, but pleased. There are the handshakes from the judges, handshakes between competitors. He is escorted to the front of the stage to pose for photos. Everyone is on their feet.

An hour later, we are still outside the artists' entrance waiting for Flynn. Professor Kaiser has gone back inside to try and fish him out. As usual there are press interviews and photographs, which always take ages. Kate is lying on the low wall, her head in Harry's lap. I am sitting on the steps, looking out into the street, counting the passers-by. After what seems like an age, the professor comes back out to say that Flynn is on his way. After another boring half-hour, Flynn finally emerges.

'Whey-hey!' Harry slaps him on the back and Kate leaps forward to hug him.

'You deserved it, you were *so* the best!' she exclaims.

'You came alive in that final movement! I think it was your greatest performance yet!' Professor Kaiser enthuses.

'You blew the competition away. It was no contest!' Harry raves.

Flynn looks flushed and sweaty from all the attention.

His eyes look past the others, searching beyond them. I hang back, suddenly uncertain, suddenly empty and afraid. If Flynn is told that he has never played better, if he is told he blew the opposition away, what chance is there he will ever start taking his lithium again?

Chapter Thirteen

FLYNN

I am relieved to finally get out of the building, away from the cameras and journalists and judges and other competitors, and back to my friends. It's always the same when you win a big competition. You just want to go home and savour the feeling, but suddenly there are all these strangers who come up and shake your hand and talk about your performance, acting like long-lost friends. We walk Professor Kaiser to his hotel and then take the bus back to Harry's – we are spending one more night there before catching the Eurostar back to London in the morning.

Harry and Kate are ebullient, advising me on ways to spend the money, but Jennah seems strangely withdrawn. Normally she would have run up to me and given me a hug and a kiss as soon as she saw me, but this time she doesn't. I feel kind of hurt. She seems distant somehow, pensive, almost sad, and it breaks my heart. She has been strangely on edge this whole trip. I sense there is something bothering her, but she doesn't seem to want to talk to me.

On our way back to London the following morning she is still the same, only talking when asked a question, otherwise sitting back, hugging her coat around her as if she is cold, barely teetering on the edge of our little group. Harry and Kate don't seem to notice, or if they do, they purposefully don't comment, just chattering on with me regardless. I find myself filled with an energy, a joy, a sense of purpose to my life that I don't remember having since winning my last major competition seven months ago. It is wonderful to reclaim that feeling.

We arrive home sometime after noon and the flat seems smaller, brighter, than when we left it. The idea of practice once again makes me fizz with excitement, and within minutes there are people calling to congratulate me – Rami, my parents, friends from the RCM. I lie with my legs hanging off the end of the sofa, chatting on the phone, while Jennah unpacks and puts a wash on, moving soundlessly through the flat. When I finally hang up the phone, I leap up and envelop her in a bear hug but she only pushes me off and tells me I smell. So I go and have a shower, returning ten minutes later in boxer shorts and wet hair, only to find her poring over books at her desk. I try to distract her by kissing her neck.

She wriggles away. 'Flynn, not now.'

'I'm not doing anything, I just want to kiss you!' I exclaim, the hurt sounding in my voice.

She goes back to her books. 'Well, I'm trying to study. Finals are in three weeks in case you'd forgotten.'

'That's ages!' I sweep the books off and plonk myself down on the desk in front of her. 'Study *me,* I'm far more interesting!'

She gets up and starts picking her books off the floor.

'Hey!' I protest.

She ignores me so I pounce on her, tickling her and wrestling her to the ground.

'Flynn, get off!'

'You wanna fight? I'll give you a fight!' I laugh, pulling her down on top of me.

'I said, *get off*!' She pulls away angrily and I am forced to let go. Her cheeks are flushed and she looks suddenly furious. I prop myself up on my elbows and blow the hair out of my eyes. 'What's got into you?' I ask in bewilderment.

She stares at me for a moment, breathing hard. 'Would you lie to me?' she demands abruptly.

'Of course not!' I exclaim, reaching out to try and tickle her foot. 'I would never lie to you. You're my soul mate, the love of my life—' I break off suddenly as I catch sight of her face.

'You really expect me to believe that?' she suddenly shouts.

I sit up, feeling the smile die on my lips. 'Jennah, what on earth . . .?'

She shakes her head, as if in disgust, and walks out of the room.

I catch up with her in the bedroom and force her round to look at me. 'What have I done?' My voice rises.

'You know what you've done! You've lied to me! You systematically lied to me for months and months!' she yells, the anger hot in her cheeks.

I start to feel frightened, even though I don't understand. 'Jennah, you're crazy, I haven't lied about anything – what the hell are you on about?'

'Oh yeah?' she shouts. 'Oh yeah?' She turns and disappears down the hall into the bathroom, returning moments later with a drawer from the medicine cabinet. 'Then what the hell are these?' she yells, emptying the contents of the drawer onto the carpet.

I stare down at the eight sealed packets of lithium carbonate I have been cramming into the drawer for the past couple of months and my heart literally stops. There is a long silence. I feel like all the breath has exited my body.

'Oh shit.'

'Yeah, that's right, oh shit.' Sparks fly from her eyes. 'Oh shit, the stupid girlfriend's finally found out.'

I feel myself flinch. 'Jennah, listen, I can explain . . .'

'Don't bother,' she says quietly. 'You weren't going to before, so what's the point?'

I can feel my heart thudding painfully in my chest. I hold up my hand. 'No, no, listen. I had a problem, with my playing—'

'You told me it wasn't a problem,' she says. 'You told me the hand tremor was just a minor inconvenience. So you were lying about that too?'

'Listen,' I say desperately. 'I didn't want to worry you—'

'That's not true, is it?' she shouts, her eyes blazing. 'That's not true either. You didn't tell me because you didn't want me to try and persuade you to keep taking your meds!'

She is right, of course. I stare at her like a rabbit caught in headlights. I say nothing.

'Flynn, after everything we've been through.' Jennah's voice is flat, emotionless. 'I can't believe it.'

'I don't need the lithium,' I hear myself say. 'It's been two whole months and I'm managing fine without it. The bipolar diagnosis was a mistake. I just have mood swings from time to time, like everyone else—'

'Oh my God!' Jennah looks like she is trying to pull her hair out. 'What the fuck are you talking about? Five months ago you tried to commit suicide!'

'I'm just a depressive then. All I need are the anti-depressants and I'm still taking those—'

'You go completely manic too! What about the paint? What about the first time I came to visit you in the psychiatric hospital? What about two nights ago at Harry's parents'?'

'What are you talking about?'

'You were horrible to me!' Jennah shouts, her face on fire. 'Even though I was dying with embarrassment, you were going on and on, laughing at me, making me out to be some kind of neurotic bitch, grossly exaggerating everything!'

'Hey,' I protest. 'But that was funny—'

'Only to you! That's what you're like when you're manic! You're only aware of your own feelings, never of others'! Everyone was embarrassed, I was practically in tears, and you just kept on and on and on!' Her anger frightens me. 'You were so wrapped up in yourself you didn't even notice when I ran out on dinner, and it was Harry who had to come after me!'

'I thought – I thought you'd gone to the loo or something—'

'No you didn't!' Jennah yells. 'You didn't think anything. Because the only person you care about when you're manic is *you*!'

I stare at her. For a moment it feels like she hates me.

She sits down on the end of the bed. Suddenly she looks exhausted. 'I'm so tired, Flynn. I'm tired of the ups and the downs and the hospitalizations and the lies . . . You don't know what it was like, seeing you in that hospital bed, wondering whether you would ever wake up, wondering which would be worse – for you to be brain-damaged or for you to be dead!' She bites her lip and her eyes fill up. 'I can't take this any more!'

I feel my heart beat faster. 'OK, OK,' I say quickly. 'I'll go back on the lithium if it means so much to you.'

'It's not only that, Flynn. I need to know that I can trust you, that you're going to be straight with me, that you're not going to try and take me for a fool. I need to trust you to talk to me about things like the side-effects – and not just to Sophie because she's a doctor—'

'But she's a neurologist,' I say. 'I thought she might be able to help me.'

'But just because I'm not a doctor doesn't mean you can't talk to me too! I have a right to be involved, Flynn. Because I care about you, because I worry about you, and because I too have to put up with a lot of the shit stuff.'

I go over to the end of the bed and sit down beside her. 'I know you do,' I say, taking her hands in mine. 'I know you do and I'm sorry. I promise, I really promise I'll be straight with you from now on. Please, please trust me again.'

She puts her arms around me. 'I love you, you fool. I just want you to be well and happy. And lithium keeps you well, Flynn. You know it does.'

That evening I intend to start taking my lithium again. I really do. I stand in front of the bathroom sink, the small white pill held between my finger and thumb. I look at it and think how tomorrow I will be feeling normal again. The white-hot energy will have left my muscles and my hands will feel twitchy and trembly as soon as I sit down at the piano. And then another thought occurs to me. The Queen Charlotte. No way would I have won that competition if I'd still been taking the meds. And in two months' time there is another competition, the Leeds International, even bigger than the last. Without the lithium I have a chance of winning it, I know I do. Winning major competitions straight out of university is crucial if you are to make a name for yourself on the concert circuit. And without the meds I can win them all, I really can. Suddenly I realize that Jennah isn't inside my head; she doesn't know. She just apes what the doctors say – *You must keep taking your lithium, you must keep taking your lithium* – because she thinks that because they are doctors they must be right. But only I know what I can and cannot achieve. At the end of the day, it's all in the mind – quite literally. I am sure I can control the bipolar disorder, I just have to figure out a way. I know there is a way, there *must* be a way. Winning the competition last night was effortless and fun. Playing like I am now, there is nothing I cannot accomplish, no title that is out of my reach. All I have to do to beat the bipolar is to exercise some powerful mind-control. I can do it, I *can*. And when I succeed, Jennah will be happy. She will be so happy to have a boyfriend who is the best concert pianist in the world and whose mind isn't slowed down by drugs. I'll make it work. I *will*.

Every evening I resume taking the three small white pills out of the blister packet. For the first few evenings Jennah hovers in the bathroom to check. But I slide them under my tongue and then spit them down the sink as I finish brushing my teeth. It is that easy. And the white-hot energy remains.

Finals pass in a crazy blur. I don't sleep much because I don't need to, and also because I find it hard to stay in one position for long. I spend most of the day cramming – as usual I have left it all till the last moment – and most of the night practising. Professor Kaiser has entered me for the Tchaikovsky competition. If I reach the finals – *when* I reach the finals – I get to fly out to Moscow. If I can win that one, my career will be launched. I have already started getting concert bookings for next year on the back of the Queen Charlotte, and Professor Kaiser has been acting as my agent.

Jennah, Harry and Kate organize study sessions together, but they seem reluctant to have me around, apparently because of my finger-tapping and knee-jiggling. I know that Jennah is regularly checking the lithium in the drawer of the medicine cabinet, but as I systematically take out the pills every evening and wash them down the sink, she is not worried. The anti-depressants stop me from going down like before, and the mania I control by myself. It's great. Gives me a real sense of power. Especially as I'm fooling everyone. Even Jennah. Of course, I will tell her eventually. But only when I have proven beyond all reasonable doubt that I can keep the bipolar under control. Professor Kaiser comments on a spectacular improvement in my playing. I only wonder why I didn't think of washing the pills down the sink before.

The feeling of release as I walk out of my last exam is tremendous. Results are still two months away but the sense of freedom is overpowering. I spin Jennah round and round until she begs me to stop. Harry and Kate join us and we are all laughing with relief, slapping each other on the back and yelling, 'No more lectures!' 'No more historical studies!' 'No more transcendental theory!' into the warm spring air. We rush home to shower and change.

The party is in a basement bar in Covent Garden. It is packed with finalists, a heaving mass of bodies and noise. Music pounds over the top of it all, glitter balls sparkle and fluorescent lights flash. The energy is palpable, the air hot and heavy with the smell of alcohol, cigarette smoke and perfume. Harry, taller than everyone else, shouts over people's heads and high-fives various mates. People I don't even recognize come up to congratulate me about the Queen Charlotte. I can't seem to stop grinning – normally a party like this would give me the heaves, but tonight I can't think of anywhere I would rather be than right here in this crowd, laughing, shouting, bursting with joy. Jennah, holding my hand, looks exquisite in a strappy black dress and heels. A single pearl on a silver necklace nestles against the curve of her collarbone and the earrings I gave her for Christmas sparkle against her hair. I am wearing chinos and a pale-blue shirt with the sleeves rolled up, my hair spiked up, and I know we are getting noticed for being such a great-looking couple. After yelling with various people over the beat of the music until my voice is hoarse, I finally manage to manoeuvre Jennah over to the dance floor. She pretends to be reluctant, but I pull her firmly by the hand and we dance amidst the jostling, laughing, gyrating crowd. The music continues to pound, the beat vibrating through the soles of our shoes, and I pull her close to me, kissing her neck, her cheek, her mouth. She laughs and draws back to look at me, her eyes very bright.

'I guess this is it! We're finally grown-ups!' she yells in my ear.

'I know! What the hell are we going to do now?' I yell back.

'You're going to be famous and I'll be your groupie!' Jennah laughs.

'Let's go round the world!' I shout.

'You really will be going round the world! Next year you'll be on your concert tour!'

'Come with me!' I shout back. 'Promise me you'll come with me to every concert and competition?'

Jennah laughs. 'What about a job? I need to earn money!'

'No you don't!' I shout back. 'I'll share my prize money with you! And there'll be a lot of it! We'll be rich!'

Jennah laughs and shakes her head in disbelief.

'You'll see!' I yell. 'You'll see! You'll see!'

We share a cab home with Harry and Kate at three in the morning. Jennah is walking barefoot and my shirt is damp with sweat. When we get out of the taxi, the birds are already singing. We wave goodbye to Harry and Kate, who are off on holiday together the very next day, and trip up the steps to our front door. Inside the flat,

Jennah drops her shoes to the floor and limps into the living room, collapsing onto the sofa.

'Coffee?' I ask.

'Yes please.' She curls up against a cushion.

I head to the kitchen, hitting the flashing answerphone button as I exit the room. Pouring water into the kettle, I hear Rami's magnified voice wishing me good luck for the last exam. A long beep, followed by Jennah's mum wishing her the same thing. Another long beep. I take two mugs off the plate rack.

'*Hello, this is a message for Flynn Laukonen from the Bridge Medical Surgery. You didn't turn up again for your blood test yesterday, and according to our records you've not been in since the twenty-eighth of March.*' I drop the kettle into the sink. '*As I'm sure you know, it's very important that you have your lithium levels checked regularly to ensure . . .*' I career into the living room and hit the off button with such force that the machine falls to the floor with a crash. I stare down at the broken machine, my heart pounding, breathing hard.

Jennah hasn't moved from the sofa. Perhaps she is asleep. Oh, please God, let her be asleep. I squat down and quietly start gathering up the broken pieces of machine.

Jennah pulls herself slowly to a sitting position, pushing her hair out of her eyes. She looks at me, sitting on the floor, surrounded by bits of broken answerphone. Her eyes are wide with shock.

'That was a mistake,' I hear myself say. My voice is

shaking. 'They – they made a mistake. I *did* go for the blood test . . .'

Jennah is breathing hard. 'You liar. Oh, you *liar*. You never did start taking your lithium again, did you?'

My heart starts to pound. 'OK, Jennah, listen. I was going to tell you. Only it didn't seem like a very good idea just before the exams and—'

'That's why you've been so hyper recently! And I was worried sick that the lithium had stopped working!'

'I was going to tell you,' I say again. 'But – but I wanted to wait until I could show you that – that I didn't need it. And I don't need it, I don't—'

'No! No! No!' Jennah starts to shout. 'Not again! We can't have this conversation again!'

'Shh,' I say desperately. 'We'll wake the neighbours.'

'I don't care about the bloody neighbours!' Jennah yells. 'I care about the fact that you lied to me, *again*, after promising, *promising* you wouldn't lie to me any more!'

'I know, but I was going to tell you—'

'All that crap about being straight with me from now on! You were just laughing at me when you were saying it! You were just laughing at me behind my back, knowing full well you had no intention of going back on the lithium. You just thought I would never be able to find out so long as you took three tablets out of the packet every day!'

'It wasn't like that—'

'You must think I'm such an idiot! You must think

you can lie to me about anything! What else have you lied about? What else have you been doing behind my back?' She has absolutely lost it. I have never seen her so angry. Her cheeks are crimson, her eyes flashing darts.

'Nothing, Jennah, I—'

'All that crap about me being your soul mate. All that crap about you being in love with me and—'

'It wasn't crap, Jennah, I *do* love you!'

'How can I believe you?' she yells. 'How am I ever supposed to believe anything you say to me ever again?'

'You can believe me. I only lied about this. I *promise*—'

'You promise?' Jennah scoffs. 'What the hell's that supposed to mean?'

'Just listen . . .' I try to approach her.

'No!' she shouts. 'Don't come near me! I don't want you near me!'

I stop. She puts her hands over her face and breathes deeply. 'OK, OK, now think . . .'

She is talking to herself. It frightens me. It's as if I am no longer present. I take a step forwards and touch her arm. 'Jennah . . .'

'No!' Her hand shoots out, pushing me away. 'I want you to leave me alone! It's my life too!'

I try and grasp her hands. 'Jennah . . .'

'Oh my God!' she shouts. 'You have got to give me space! Otherwise *I'm* the one who's going to go crazy!'

'OK, OK.' I step back quickly. 'I'm giving you space.'

She drops her hands. 'No, I need space.' Her voice

drops suddenly. '*Real* space.' She breathes deeply and her eyes meet mine.

'OK, let's sit down and talk about it,' I suggest.

'No,' Jennah says. 'We did that last time. You just fed me a lot of bullshit, told me what you thought I wanted to hear . . .' She screws her eyes up tight. 'I need a break. I need to actually be away from you.'

'You don't,' I say quickly. 'You don't. We just need to talk this through—'

'I need a break, Flynn!' Her eyes suddenly fill with tears. 'Don't you get it? I need to be apart from you for a while.'

I stare at her in horror. 'You're breaking up with me?'

'I don't know.' She looks stunned, exhausted. 'Yes, maybe that's what we need. Maybe we need to break up for a while.'

I glare at her in disbelief. 'For a while or for ever?' I challenge her furiously.

'I don't know, Flynn. But definitely for now.' She shakes her head, tears hanging on her lashes. 'I'm sorry.'

She turns and leaves the room, disappearing down the corridor towards the bedroom. I feel a cold wave of shock wash over me and for several moments I cannot move. Then my heart starts to thump as if it's about to explode and I realize I must do something, anything, to stop her from walking out of the flat. In the bedroom she has a suitcase open on the bed. Dawn is already streaming through the open curtains. She is emptying the cupboard of her clothes, not even bothering to take them off the hangers, just tossing them straight into the open suitcase.

'Jennah, stop.' I put my arm around her to try and restrain her. 'This is crazy.'

'Flynn,' she says, her voice shaking, 'I asked you not to touch me. Either you let me pack, or I'm calling Harry to come and fetch me.'

I step back. 'Don't call Harry,' I say quickly.

'Fine. Then let me pack.'

I move away from her and sit down on the edge of the bed. 'Jennah, I really think you're over-reacting. I don't think us breaking up is the answer.' I wish my voice would stop shaking.

She doesn't reply and starts attacking the drawers. Within minutes, the bedroom is empty of her clothes. She grabs her sports bag off the top of the wardrobe and disappears into the living room, then into the bathroom. When she returns, the bag is full.

'Where are you going to go?' I challenge her. 'It's barely even daylight!'

She doesn't answer. She zips up the suitcase, pulls on a pair of jeans over her party dress, and shoves on her trainers. Then she pulls out her mobile phone and dials a number. She orders a minicab and gives our address. She asks to be taken to Euston station. She is going home.

'Come on, this is silly . . .' I try and wrestle the mobile from her but she pushes me away. She snaps it shut and pulls on her jacket, taking her keys out of the pocket and laying them on the desk.

She stops and her eyes meet mine. 'I'm sorry, Flynn.' The anger has left her. A wave of sheer panic rushes through me.

'You've got to be kidding me.' I can hear my voice rising. 'You *can't* be breaking up with me!'

She picks up the bag and grasps the handle of the suitcase, pulling it along on its wheels. 'I've got to go, Flynn. They said the cab would be here in five minutes.'

'Jennah, please. Would you just listen . . .?' I grab her arm, feeling a rush of heat in my eyes.

Her bottom lip quivers. 'I need you to let go of me, Flynn.'

'Please don't, Jen!' I have started crying but I don't care.

She bites her lip hard. 'You're going to be OK,' she says. 'Go and stay with Rami, all right?'

'Jennah, please, I'm begging you!'

There is the sound of a car horn from the street outside. Jennah pulls away as a tear glances off, her cheek. 'Bye, Flynn.'

The front door clicks closed behind her. I can hear her wrestling with the suitcase on the stairs. Moments later the downstairs door bangs shut and there are voices in the street below. I get up off the sofa and rush over to the window. As I look down, I see the doors of the minicab slam closed. The engine starts, and the car glides down the street and out of sight.

I turn from the window and sink slowly to a sitting position against the wall. *OK, OK, calm down,* I tell myself. *It's going to be all right. She's going to come back, isn't she?* Except that she isn't. I am going to die, I realize. I am actually going to die. I put my hands over my face and start to sob. I feel like I am being slowly, carefully, ripped in two. I realize that this pain is worse than anything I could ever imagine. Worse than the deepest depression. I can hardly breathe with the strength of it. I feel sure that pain of this intensity cannot be sustained: any minute I will pass out. But I don't, and the pain keeps on growing, fresh waves of undiluted agony. I am sobbing so hard I can barely draw breath. My lungs feel as if they are ready to burst and the gasping, retching noises make me sound as if I am suffocating.

Fear courses through my veins. Fear and pain, in equal doses. She has to come back. She simply *has* to come back. I cannot live without her. I cannot, and I *will* not. So this is what they mean about dying of a broken heart. It is actually possible. I lie down on the carpet. I want to knock myself out; I really wish I could knock myself out. The sobs rack my body as if I am being brutally shaken. Every muscle aches with exhaustion and soon the carpet, my hands, my face, my shirtsleeves – everything is soaked.

I lift my head from my arms and look up at the room through a thick fog. *She is not going to come back,* I tell myself. *You are going to live the rest of your life without her. You are not going to propose to her, you are not going to marry her, you are not going to have children with her, you are not going to grow old with her. Maybe you will never even see her again. You will never again hold her, never again stroke her cheek, never again smell her hair or feel her kiss. You should have really, really paid more attention when you made love to her last night, because it was your last time. You really should have savoured that last kiss at the party, just a few hours ago. Never again, never again. Never.*

I am tormenting myself and gaining a savage satisfaction from it. I want to hurt myself more, stab myself in the wound, break down my horrible self. I sink my teeth into the side of my hand and bite down as hard as I can. I taste blood. But the physical pain doesn't even begin to dent the mental one. I cry until I can barely move. I cry until the sun outside is high in the sky. I drag my aching self over to the sofa and continue crying into the cushions. I go to the bathroom and splash my face with cold water and still can't stop the tears.

Beside the basin, something catches my attention. The bottom drawer of the medicine cabinet is slightly open. I wrench it out and see that all my meds have been removed. All but a single blister strip of lithium and a single strip of anti-depressants and four benzodiazepines. All the rest are gone. Confused, I rifle through the other drawers of the cabinet. All the aspirin has gone, all the paracetamol. So that's what she was doing with the sports bag. Emptying the flat of pills so that I wouldn't kill myself. I want to laugh. *You're so stupid,* I want to say. *There are kitchen knives, aren't there?*

Windows that open? Glasses which can be broken? Do you honestly think that by taking away all the pills you will somehow stop me from killing myself? Then another thought occurs to me. That in her hurt, angry state, Jennah still had the presence of mind to do this. *Don't kill yourself,* she says to me through the empty drawer. *Don't kill yourself over me.*

I feel like everything inside me has shattered, every part of me has broken into a thousand tiny pieces that I will never be able to put back together again. I stagger into the bedroom and throw myself down on the unmade bed. Her pillow still holds traces of her smell. I jump up, look around wildly for something that belongs to her. I find a T-shirt of hers on the floor. I lie back down and rub it against my wet, burning cheek like a comfort blanket, inhaling her gentle odour. I close my eyes and try to pretend she is still beside me.

The shrill ring of the phone drags me from a deep, foggy sleep, and I wake shivering, cold and disorientated. The room is filled with darkness. The bedside alarm reads ten to nine. The phone continues to ring. I want to leave it, but what if it's Jennah? Jennah, calling to say she is on her way back? I grab the receiver and press it to my ear. 'Hello?'

'Hello, Flynn.' Not Jennah. Sophie. I close my eyes against the disappointment.

'Hi.'

'Lovey, Jen called and told me what happened. I'm going to come and pick you up, OK?'

I can't let anyone see me like this. 'No, don't. It's all right. I'm OK.' My voice shakes.

'I'm still going to come and pick you up,' Sophie says. 'I'm leaving now. Rami's working tonight. Throw some clothes into a bag and meet me outside when I beep, OK? I'll have Aurora in the back so I won't be able to come up.'

'No, Sophie, listen, I don't feel like seeing anyone right now—'

'See you in half an hour,' Sophie says, and she hangs up.

I put down the phone and look around in panic. Oh no, no, no, this is the last thing I want. Sophie driving all the way from Watford to fetch me. With Aurora in tow. I pick up the phone and press call-back. The phone just rings and rings.

Sometime later a car horn sounds from the street below. I contemplate not answering but then remember that Rami and Sophie have a spare key. Shoving on my trainers, I go reluctantly down into the street.

Sophie is double parked with her hazards on, Aurora asleep in the car seat. As soon as I come out, Sophie gets back into the car.

'Soph, I'm not coming.'

She ignores me and opens the passenger door. A car comes up behind her and honks irritably. Sophie winds down her window and looks at me, waiting. With a sigh of despair, I go back upstairs, grab my jacket, lock up the flat and come back down into the street. The driver in the car behind has opened his door and is now swearing at Sophie. I slam the front door closed and quickly get into the car. As soon as I do so, Sophie puts her foot down.

'Horrible man,' she says, and flashes me a smile.

'Sophie, I really don't need you to do this,' I say. 'I'm perfectly OK.'

'So? Is it a crime for me to want to see my favourite brother-in-law?'

I manage a painful smile.

'Put your seatbelt on,' she tells me.

I do as she asks. 'Jennah shouldn't have called you,' I say.

'And it's lovely to see you too,' Sophie replies with a wink.

Chapter Fourteen

JENNAH

I am shaking all the way up to Manchester. Shaking with fear at what I have done, shaking with horror, shaking with cold. The image of Flynn standing in the hallway, his face shocked, his gaze imploring, is etched into my brain. The anger has faded now and is replaced only by a desperate sense of loss, of loneliness, of betrayal. Although my trust in him has been shattered, my love for him is still acute, a stab of red-hot pain through my heart. I know I am running away from more than just the lies; I am running away from the non-medicated Flynn, the bipolar Flynn, the two faces like the opposite sides of a coin. I think of the waxwork Flynn in the hospital bed and know that it is him, more than anything else, that I am running from now. I wanted some assurances that my life would never again be torn apart like that, that I would never again suffer the pain of watching my loved one destroyed by his own hand. And with that one telephone message I realized, in a brutal, final way, that so long as I was with Flynn I would never be protected from the horror of suicide. That he would always be capable of stopping his medication, always be capable of lying to cover his illness, always be capable of swallowing forty pills and lying down beside his girlfriend to die.

I stare out of the grimy window, motionless, numb. When the train pulls into Manchester, it takes me several moments to recognize my stop. I stumble off the train, dragging my suitcase and bag behind me, and stagger out into the car park, my eyes searching for the white Nissan. When I see Mum, I drop everything and throw my arms around her and burst into tears. 'Don't say it!' I beg. 'Just don't say it! Don't say I told you so!'

She drives me home and makes me have a hot bath and feeds me soup and listens to me bawl out the whole story. She doesn't say I told you so but she does say that I've done the right thing, which only makes me cry harder. She does her best to listen, does her best to sound sympathetic, but in her eyes I can read how relieved she is now that I have left him. And I understand why, even if it makes me want to scream.

We watch *The Simpsons* and she tells me how a boy broke her heart when she was seventeen. I listen, to please her, to make her think she is helping. Her partner, Alan, pats me on the back and says some kind words. I go to bed early and stare at my mobile phone, willing it to ring. I want to call Flynn so badly my fingers ache. I call Rami instead. He is not there. I tell Sophie what happened. I ask her to look after Flynn for me and then hang up before I start to cry again.

I lie in bed, staring at the darkness. The hours crawl by. I cannot sleep. I look at my watch and see that it is nearly eleven. By now Sophie will have gone round to the flat like she said she would, will have somehow persuaded Flynn to go back with her to the house in Watford. I think of Flynn, in the guest room at Rami's, and try to imagine what he is thinking, what he is feeling. I honestly wonder whether it is possible to die of pain.

The rest of the week passes in a painful fog. I am running a temperature, I don't want to leave my bed, I refuse to eat anything sensible – only biscuits and ice cream. I shout at Mum when she tries to open the curtains. I watch hours of daytime TV. In desperation, my mother persuades the doctor to come round and he diagnoses tonsillitis. I wish it was something more serious. At the end of the week my temperature drops. I haven't showered for five days and the bedroom looks like a tip. I take a bath and wash my hair, stuff all the junk into a bin bag, vacuum the room, then tell my mother I am going out to look for a job. I spend the next three hours walking aimlessly around the city with tears in my eyes. I want to give up and lie down here on the pavement. I don't want to go through the rest of my life without Flynn.

Mum and I start getting on each other's nerves. 'I just wish you would do something productive,' she says. 'You need to think of your career – teacher training, if you're still interested – but as usual you've left it all till the last minute and now you're finding yourself with nothing to do.'

'I said I'd register with an employment agency,' I say between gritted teeth, trying to read the paper at the kitchen counter. 'What more do you want?'

'I want you to do something you enjoy,' Mum persists. 'I don't see you working in an office. You've done four years of music training – surely there is something you could do where you could use your talent and your musical skills?'

'We can't all be concert pianists like Flynn,' I point out acidly.

'I'm not suggesting you become a concert pianist,' Mum says, with infuriating calm. 'What about that Frenchwoman you met at your last recital? Didn't she want to take you on as a pupil? You always said you wanted to study abroad, and the Paris Conservatoire has an excellent reputation.'

'I've already said no,' I snap.

'But didn't she ask you to think about it?' Mum persists. 'Didn't she say you would have a shot at a scholarship and be able to combine voice study with a practical teaching qualification?'

'I am *not* going to live in Paris!' I exclaim.

'Why?' Mum challenges me. 'Because of Flynn? Darling, you're too young to throw your life away on some guy – some guy with a serious mental illness, who clearly will never be able to make you happy—'

'Just leave Flynn out of this, OK?' I storm from the room, my vision blurring with unfallen tears. I sit on the edge of my bed and press the tips of my fingers against my eyelids. Why doesn't he ring? *Why doesn't he ring?*

On Saturday morning Mum appears in my room before I've even had a chance to get out of bed. 'Darling, listen, it's rather important.'

I sit up, my heart thudding. Flynn?

'You remember your old singing teacher, Mrs Ellis? Well, I bumped into her at the supermarket just now and she's organizing her yearly charity concert, in support of the NSPCC. Do you remember – you used to take part in it every year? Well, she was so excited to hear that you were back, because one of her sopranos has dropped out with laryngitis and the concert is less than two weeks away—'

'Mum, no!' I brush the hair out of my eyes and squint against the morning light. 'I am *not* going to stand in the church hall and sing *Morning Has Broken* for the benefit of Mrs Ellis and her cronies!'

'Darling, listen. It's much more upmarket than that. They're actually performing at the Dewey Hall and more than five hundred people are due to attend. Oh, come on, love. Mrs Ellis has been so good to you over the years. She helped you prepare for the Royal College audition – in fact, if I remember correctly, she was the one who suggested you take voice as your second—'

'OK, OK,' I snap. 'Don't go on. What song do I have to sing?'

'Anything you want,' Mum says eagerly. 'It's the last piece in the recital and they'll change the programme just for you.'

I think of the score of *Letting Go,* hidden under a pile of clothes in my suitcase. 'Fine. I hope the accompanist is a quick learner because he won't have come across this one before.'

Chapter Fifteen

FLYNN

I am back on the lithium. My plan is very simple. Do everything I'm supposed to do. Keep taking the meds, regain some kind of mental equilibrium and then go and find Jennah. But I need to wait at least a month. I need to show her I've been back on the meds for a month if I'm to have a chance of getting her to trust me again.

Rami and Sophie won't let me go back to the flat. They help me with the rent and insist I stay in their guest room. It's been twelve days and four hours. This is the longest I've been parted from Jennah since we started going out. I don't recognize myself without her. I seem to have forgotten who I am. Every day I have to fight the urge to board a train to Manchester. I have to remind myself that the only way I'm going to prove to her that I'm serious about taking the lithium is with time. But the hours slow to a crawl.

I don't leave the house. Sophie starts to worry. Rami is working crazy shifts at the hospital so I spend most of my time with her and the baby. I offer to babysit but

Sophie doesn't seem to want to leave me on my own. I work my way through their entire collection of DVDs.

I play with Aurora while Sophie prepares dinner. I sit on the living-room rug, leaning against the foot of the sofa, knees drawn up, as Aurora toddles happily back and forth to her toy box, bringing me her favourite toys. She is looking more like a little girl and less like a baby now – her blonde curls cover the nape of her neck and her face is losing that chubby look. During the course of the afternoon she has somehow managed to lose her trousers and is now waddling about in her T-shirt and nappy, her eyes bright with concentration. She plants her feet firmly apart and bends down to place a ball on the carpet in front of me, then claps her hands and staggers backwards, ready to play. I roll the ball gently over to her and she flies into a flurry of excitement, tottering after it and sending it rolling even further away in her desire to catch it. As I watch her play, a sharp, shocking thought occurs to me. Maybe Jennah is happier now. Maybe now that she is away from my moods, away from the arguments, away from the threat of hospitals, she is finally able to put herself first and focus on her own life. Maybe the argument about the lithium was actually a blessing in disguise – maybe it offered her a way out. I vividly remember the expression on her face as she approached my hospital bedside after I came round – she looked white, shell-shocked, terrified. And I remember Rami telling me later how much she cried – sobbed – when she realized I was going to be OK. Later there was the period when she kept having nightmares and told me she was afraid I was going to try and kill myself again. And of course there was the Christmas present, the theatre tickets that I never even looked at because I was so consumed by my own despair. I found the still-sealed envelope months later, after I came back from hospital, when I was emptying the pockets of her clothes to put on a wash. She never said anything about that unopened present; there were never any recriminations, never any anger. She just accepted it without complaint, the way she accepted the painting episode and the suicide attempt, and hid her tears from me. But now – now she is free. Free to lead her own life, free to move on. Just because I can't live without her doesn't mean she can't live without me.

The thoughts don't leave me alone. At night I can't sleep. I get up and roam the house. Watch television with the sound muted. Go into the kitchen and drink milk straight from the bottle. One night, Sophie surprises me. 'I've only just got Aurora back to sleep and now you!' She closes the kitchen door, pads over to the cupboard in her nightdress and hands me a glass.

'Thanks.' I sit down at the kitchen table, resting my feet on the stool in front. Sophie puts on the kettle and joins me at the table. 'You,' she says seriously, 'have got to get some sleep.'

I look across at her. I am so tired, I feel sick. I start to chew my thumbnail.

'I think we're going to have to put you on a short course of sleeping pills,' Sophie says.

'Maybe now I'm an insomniac as well as a manic-depressive,' I mutter.

'I think what you are, lovey, is stressed.'

I manage a wry smile. 'I'm not exactly leading a very stressful life.'

'I think you're stressed that what happened between you and Jennah is irreparable. And I think you're wrong.'

I take a deep breath and look at Sophie. 'Maybe it shouldn't be repaired,' I say slowly. 'Maybe it would be best for Jennah if it wasn't. She worries about the future, you know. Late at night, when I'm practising, she goes on the Internet and reads up everything she can on bipolar disorder. She even printed out some stuff too – I found it hidden in her desk drawer. Stuff like children having a thirty per cent chance of inheriting bipolar from their parents, and people with bipolar spending a quarter of their lives in hospital—'

'It's good that she's aware of some of the statistics,' Sophie says, 'and it's good that she's keeping herself informed. And there is the small possibility she *has* decided that it's all too much of a risk. But, Flynn, you won't know until you talk to her.'

'Maybe – maybe the whole lithium fight was just an excuse,' I say. 'She didn't want to admit she was breaking up with me because of the bipolar, so instead she made out she was breaking up with me because I'd lied.'

There is a silence. I rip off a narrow strip of fingernail with my teeth. 'I'm starting to think – I'm starting to think she really might be happier without me.' A sharp pain rises up behind my eyes and I look away.

Sophie says nothing for a moment. 'She loves you, Flynn. I'm sure of that.'

'Perhaps, but that doesn't mean I can make her happy.' My throat hurts.

'You can try,' Sophie says gently.

'I have tried. And I've failed.' I bite the corner of my lip, hard.

'You're depressed, Flynn,' Sophie says quietly. 'And when you're depressed, you always think badly of yourself.'

'But it's not the bipolar that's making me see things this way, it's the truth. I've messed up this whole year and put Jennah and my parents and Rami through hell, and I can't – I can't seem to stop. All I do is drag everyone down with me, and my family has to put up with it, but Jennah, she doesn't, she has a choice . . .' I feel a tear escape down my cheek. 'Shit—' I wipe it away angrily and sniff hard.

I feel Sophie's hand on my arm. 'It's been a difficult year. It's not always going to be like this.'

'I j-just don't seem to be able keep it together any more!' I take a deep breath and hold it. *Pull yourself together, Flynn, for Christ's sake.*

'You're back on the lithium now; you just need to give it a chance to work,' Sophie says quietly.

'But the lithium doesn't cure anything.'

'No, but it can help.'

'I just want Jennah to be happy!' I blurt out.

Sophie strokes my back. 'I know you do, love, I know you do. And you'll find a way. I'm sure about that.'

The following morning I receive a letter. A letter, addressed to me, here in Watford. My heart starts to pound. I tear it open while Sophie spoons runny egg into Aurora's open mouth.

There is nothing inside. Yes, there *is* something inside. A ticket. Huh? A concert ticket. *Charity concert in support of the NSPCC, Dewey Hall, Manchester, Saturday 18th July.* That's less than a week away. I look back at the address on the envelope. Jennah's handwriting, without a doubt.

'I don't get it,' I say to Sophie, showing it to her.

'It's an invitation to a concert,' Sophie says simply. 'Go and find out.'

'Yes, but why? Is she going to be there too?'

'I don't know,' Sophie replies, still feeding Aurora. 'But if Jennah has invited you to a concert, then I suggest that you go.'

'Why?' I am crushed that there is no letter. Just a stupid concert ticket. What is Jennah playing at?

'Don't you think it might be some kind of gesture?' Sophie asks, noticing the expression on my face.

'Gesture of what?'

'Maybe . . . a step toward reconciliation?'

'Maybe it's a joke,' I mutter. But inside, my heart is doing backflips. OK, it's not a letter, but it's still something. A sign. From Jennah. A sign she is still thinking of me.

Chapter Sixteen

JENNAH

I don't know why I sent Flynn a ticket to the concert. Well, actually that's not true, I *do* know why. Because I want him to come. I want him to come and hear me sing *Letting Go* in public for the very first time. I want him to come and see how much I still love him. But now I realize it was a mistake. It was a mistake because now, either way, I'm going to cry. If he comes, I'll cry. If he doesn't come, I'll cry even more. A lose-lose situation. And the deadliest thing you can do when trying to sing is start to cry.

My nerves are absolutely shot. It's ridiculous. Just some silly charity concert in some silly, nothing music hall in Manchester. But if Flynn comes, it will be the first time I will have seen him in eighteen days. If I manage to get through *Letting Go,* it will be the first time his song is publicly performed. And if Flynn comes to find me afterwards . . . My heart thumps as if it's ready to burst. *Please let him come. Oh, please let him come.*

I almost want to ring Sophie to check he received the ticket. What if it got lost in the post? But then I realize that ringing would defeat the whole purpose. I just have to hope. But I do hope; I hope so much it hurts.

I am doing my make-up in the large communal dressing room, amongst a dozen or so other singers, most of them pupils or friends of Mrs Ellis. The main doors have just opened and we can already hear the distant rumble of people going to their seats. Someone comes in to give us our fifteen-minute call. I feel spectacularly ill.

The black concert dress decorated with silver sequins is so thin I feel like I have nothing on. Talk about exposed. Talk about vulnerable. I can feel my knees shaking. It takes me three attempts to get my hair up. I think I might be sick.

I can hear the hum of the audience from the platform entrance, almost feel their heat. The orchestra is tuning up already. Mrs Ellis comes off the stage after giving a short speech. The first performer leaves the dressing room, and moments later I hear the sound of applause. Then the orchestral introduction to *Ave Maria*. Why did the woman I'm replacing have to be last? The seconds tick by like slow torture. I accept a cigarette from someone. Too bad if I sound like Patty Bouvier when I finally get to sing.

The recital drags on. Alice, an old school friend, is chatting to me, but all I am aware of is the frantic beating of my heart. Is he there or isn't he? Just tell me, God, and put me out of my misery. I want to rush out into the auditorium, scan the rows of seats for a sign of his tousled blond hair. He must be here. He *must.*

When I finally step out onto the stage to sing *Letting Go* at the very end of the recital, my legs threaten to buckle beneath me. I can't remember ever feeling this nervous before, not for anything. I catch sight of Mum and Alan beaming proudly in the front row. The rest of the audience is just a mass of dark heads. How will I ever know if Flynn is here or not? The applause dies away. I want to lie down and die.

The lights have been dimmed – how appropriate – and the members of the orchestra are sitting back. It is just me and the funny little balding accompanist. The music starts. Concentrate on the song. The song. Flynn's song. I take a breath and start to sing.

The applause at the end is tremendous. I'm desperate to get off the stage but Mrs Ellis forces me out for a second bow. I don't dare scan the audience. If I see Flynn now, I don't think I will be able to cope.

In the dressing room the noise and good cheer are overpowering. Everyone is laughing and jostling and chatting and back-slapping. I try to concentrate on getting my things together as quickly as I can. My hands won't stop shaking and I am being jogged from all sides. In a few minutes I will be going out of the stage door, where I am due to meet Mum and Alan. Will he be there? *Will he?*

I button my coat with fumbling fingers and step out into the cold night air. There are people, people everywhere; taxis at the kerb, performers being hugged, the streetlamps very bright. Members of the audience come up to congratulate me – a friend of Mum's, a friend of Mrs Ellis's, another friend of Mum's. Everyone is jostling, talking, laughing. I can't see Flynn anywhere. Mrs Ellis has grabbed me by the arm and is trying to introduce me to someone.

'Isn't she a star? A former pupil, no less, just back from studying at the Royal College of Music . . .'

'Really? You're not little Jennah Dawson who used to go to school with my Freddie . . .?'

'You really have a beautiful voice . . .'

'Hey, Freddie, it's Jennah Dawson!'

'That song of yours, who wrote it? It's not one I recognize . . .'

'She stepped in for Marianne just like that! It couldn't have been more perfect!'

'Do you sing professionally?'

I look at them and then suddenly past them, beyond them. I see a familiar figure lurking at the edge of the crowd. A long dark coat, tousled blond hair, a gaze so piercing it hurts. He smiles slightly and then steps away, steps back, turns away. *No.*

'Well done, darling. You sang beautifully. Didn't she sing beautifully, Alan?' Mum is hugging me now. Alan is taking my bag. Mrs Ellis is asking whether I will take part again next year . . .

The figure is moving, moving away across the street. As he reaches the other side, he turns back and looks at me. Raises his eyebrows and nods as if to say well done. Then he leaves, walking quickly down the road.

I am going to burst. I am going to burst with disappointment, sorrow and pain. I scan the street desperately with my eyes. He does not come back. *He does not come back.*

The crowd is dispersing now. Mum looks cold. 'Have you got all your things, love? Let's go then, the car's just round the corner.'

'Yes,' I say numbly. 'All right, I'm coming.'

As we approach the car, I stop and pull out my mobile. I find the crumpled business card buried deep inside my purse. I peer at it under a lamppost and force myself to key in the mobile number written across the bottom. If Flynn can just walk away, then so can I.

'Françoise Denier,' a woman's voice answers in a sharp French accent.

'It's Jennah Dawson,' I say. 'The girl who sang *Summertime* at the Royal College of Music's recital at St Martin-in-the-Fields in March.' My voice is shaking. Will she even remember me? 'I'm sorry to ring you so late, but I just wanted to say, if – if you're still interested in having me at the *conservatoire* in September, I – I'd like to accept.'

There is a silence. I can hear my heart. 'Well, this is a surprise. I am due to fly back to Paris the day after tomorrow. But I did like your voice. You had a clarity, a freshness that I have been looking for. I could perhaps see you tomorrow. I am in Oxford at the moment. Can you come here?'

'Yes, of course,' I say quickly. 'Where should I meet you?'

Using the car bonnet as a writing surface, I scribble down directions on the back of the business card with a pen hurriedly supplied by Mum. When I hang up, Mum is beaming. 'Oh, darling, I'm so glad,' she says as we get into the car. 'You've made the right decision, I'm sure of it. Alan, did you hear? Jennah's going to study singing at the Paris Conservatoire. Under the wing of a famous French opera singer! Oh, how exciting, darling. A new chapter in your life!'

I smile and nod, fighting back tears.

Chapter Seventeen

FLYNN

I walk quickly back to the station. I will not cry, I will not cry. You sang the song so beautifully, my love. Perhaps I hoped you would be a wreck, perhaps I hoped you would be a mess. But when you came out of that door, surrounded by friends and family, your eyes alight with happiness, everything became clear. Suddenly I knew what I had to do to make you happy. Suddenly I realized the answer had been there all the time.

They say that if you really love someone, you should be willing to set them free. So that is what I am doing. I will step back and you will move on. I will let you go. I will not bring you back to London, back to hospitals and moods and rows. I will watch you from a distance, watch you succeed in whatever you do. And without me, you will.

My lovely Jennah, my beautiful Jennah. Your happiness means everything to me. I will listen for your voice in the distance. I will look at the moon. I will keep you in my pocket. I will carry your smile with me everywhere, like a warm and comforting glow.